THE PASTA DETECTIVES

© Dirk Steinhöfel

Andreas Steinhöfel wurde 1962 in Battenberg geboren. Er ist Autor zahlreicher, vielfach preisgekrönter Kinder- und Jugendbücher, wie z.B. »Die Mitte der Welt«. Für »Rico, Oskar und die Tieferschatten« erhielt er u.a. den Deutschen Jugendliteraturpreis. Nach Peter Rühmkorf, Loriot, Robert Gernhardt und Tomi Ungerer hat Andreas Steinhöfel 2009 den Erich Kästner Preis für Literatur verliehen bekommen. 2013 wurde er mit dem Sonderpreis des Deutschen Jugendliteraturpreises für sein Gesamtwerk ausgezeichnet und 2017 folgte der James-Krüss-Preis. Zudem wurde er für den ALMA und den Hans-Christian-Andersen-Preis nominiert. Andreas Steinhöfel ist als erster Kinder- und Jugendbuchautor Mitglied der Deutschen Akademie für Sprache und Dichtung. Seine Serie über Rico und Oskar wurde sehr erfolgreich fürs Kino verfilmt. Zusätzlich zu seiner Autorentätigkeit arbeitet er als Übersetzer und Rezensent und schreibt Drehbücher. Seit 2015 betätigt er sich in seiner Filmfirma sad ORIGAMI als Produzent von Kinderfilmen.

© Doris Katharina Künster

Peter Schössow, Jahrgang 1953, gehört zu den renommiertesten deutschen Illustratoren. Nach seinem Studium an der Fachhochschule für Gestaltung in Hamburg arbeitete er unter anderem für Spiegel, Stern und »Die Sendung mit der Maus«. Darüber hinaus hat er eine Vielzahl von Kinderbüchern verfasst und illustriert, für die er mehrfach ausgezeichnet wurde, unter anderem mit dem Troisdorfer Bilderbuchpreis und dem Deutschen Jugendliteraturpreis. Peter Schössow lebt in Hamburg.

ANDREAS STEINHÖFEL

THE PASTA DETECTIVES

INS ENGLISCHE ÜBERSETZT
VON CHANTAL WRIGHT

MIT BILDERN VON PETER SCHÖSSOW

CARLSEN

FOR GIANNI …

FROM ME TO YOU AND BACK AGAIN

A.S.

Alle Bände über Rico und Oskar im Carlsen Verlag
(deutsche Ausgaben):

Rico, Oskar und die Tieferschatten
Rico, Oskar und das Herzgebreche
Rico, Oskar und der Diebstahlstein
Rico, Oskar und das Vomhimmelhoch
Rico, Oskar und das Mistverständnis

Wir produzieren nachhaltig

- Klimaneutrales Produkt
- Papiere aus nachhaltigen und kontrollierten Quellen
- Hergestellt in Europa

FSC
www.fsc.org
MIX
Papier | Fördert gute Waldnutzung
FSC® C021394

Veröffentlicht in der Carlsen Verlag GmbH
Völckersstraße 14-20, 22765 Hamburg
April 2023

Originaltitel: *Rico, Oskar und die Tieferschatten*

Umschlag, Illustrationen und Layout: Peter Schössow
Umschlaggestaltung: formlabor nach der Vorlage von Peter Schössow
Aus dem Deutschen von Chantal Wright
ISBN 978-3-551-32084-1

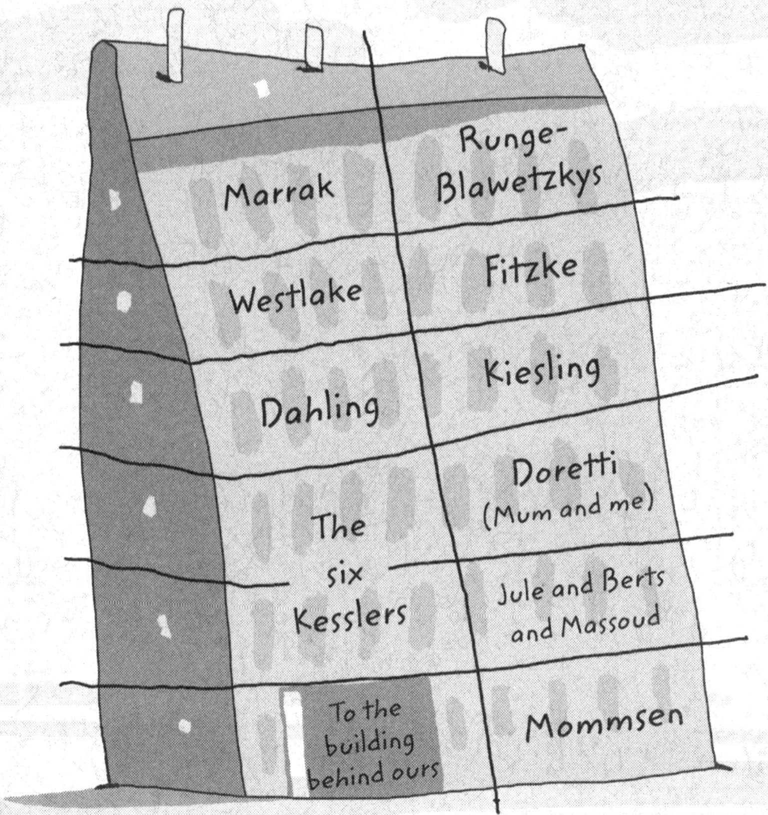

Runge-
Blawetzkys
Marrak
Fitzke
Westlake
Kiesling
Dahling
Doretti
(Mum and me)
The
six
Kesslers
Jule and Berts
and Massoud
To the
building
behind ours
Mommsen

SATURDAY

PASTA SURPRISE

The piece of pasta lay on the **pavement**. It was fat and crinkled, with a hole right through the middle. Some dried-up cheese sauce and dirt were stuck to it. I picked it up, cleaned off the dirt and looked up past the old windows of Dieffe 93 into the summer sky. Not a cloud in sight. Definitely none of those white stripes that jet engines leave behind. And besides, I thought to myself, I don't think you can just open an aeroplane window and throw out your food.

I let myself into my block of flats, whizzed up the yellow-painted stairway to the third floor and rang Mrs Dahling's bell. She had large, bright curlers in her hair, just as she did every Saturday.

»Could be rigatoni. The sauce is definitely Gorgonzola,« she declared. »It's nice of you to bring me the piece of pasta, dear, but *I* didn't throw it out of the window. Why don't you ask Mr Fitzke?«

She grinned at me, tapped one finger against her forehead, rolled her eyes and looked up at the ceiling. Mr Fitzke lives on the fourth floor. I hate him. Also, I don't think the piece of pasta is his. Mrs Dahling was my first choice because she often throws things out of the window. Last winter she threw out a television. Followed five minutes later by her husband, though he came out of the front door. After that, she came down to see us, and Mum had to pour her a drop of whisky.

---

pavement – Gehweg

»He has a girlfriend!« Mrs Dahling had exclaimed in shock. »And the stupid cow is no younger than I am! Give me another **swig** of that stuff!«

The very next day, with the telly in **smithereens** and her husband gone, she bought herself an amazing new flat-screen TV and DVD player. We sometimes watch romantic films or thrillers together, but only at the weekend when Mrs Dahling can have a lie-in. During the week she works behind the butcher's counter at a department store. Her hands are always red raw because it's so cold in there.

When we watch television we eat canapés with boiled ham and eggs or smoked salmon. If it's a romantic comedy, Mrs Dahling sniffs her way through at least ten tissues, then starts complaining about the film. »As if that sort of thing really happens! When a man and a woman get together, that's when the misery begins, but of course they never show *that* in films. What a pack of lies! Another canapé, Rico?«

»Are we still on for this evening?« Mrs Dahling called after me as I ran up to the fourth floor, two steps at a time.

»Course!«

Her door banged shut and I knocked at Mr Fitzke's. You always have to knock at Mr Fitzke's. His bell is broken. It probably has been since they built the flats in 1910.

I had to wait, wait, wait.

---

swig – Schluck

in smithereens – in Trümmern liegen

And listen to the shuffle, shuffle, shuffle behind the old wooden door.

Finally Mr Fitzke appeared, dressed, as usual, in his dark blue pyjamas with the grey stripes. His wrinkled face was covered in stubble and his stringy grey hair shot out from his head in all directions.

What a mess!

A strong smell of mould wafted out. Who knew what Mr Fitzke kept in there. In his flat, I mean, not in his head. I tried to look past him without him noticing, but he stood in my way. Deliberately! I've been in every flat in the building apart from his. Mr Fitzke won't let me in because he doesn't like me.

»Ah, the little **dimwit**,« he growled.

At this point I should explain that my name is Rico and that I am a **child proddity**. That's a bit like being a **child prodigy**, but also like the opposite. I think an awful lot, but I also need a lot of time to figure things out. There's nothing wrong with my brain, though. It's a perfectly normal size. Only sometimes a few things go missing, and unfortunately I never know when or where it's going to happen. And I can't always concentrate very well when I'm telling a story. I have a mind like a sieve – at least I think it's a sieve, it

---

dimwit – Schwachkopf

child proddity – tiefbegabtes Kind

child prodigy – hochbegabtes Kind, Wunderkind

could be a cheese grater or a **whisk** … and now you see my problem.

My head is sometimes as topsy-turvy as a barrel full of lottery balls. I play bingo every Tuesday with Mum at the *Grey* ***Bumblebees*** senior citizens' club and they have a drum full of bingo balls there which is just the same. I have no idea why mum enjoys going there so much because it really is only for pensioners. Some of them never seem to go home, because they wear the same clothes every week – just like Mr Fitzke and his one pair of pyjamas – and a few of them smell a bit funny. Maybe Mum likes it so much because she wins all the time. She beams every time she goes on stage to collect one of those cheap plastic handbags – she only ever wins cheap plastic handbags, in fact.

The pensioners don't really notice. Quite a lot of them gradually nod off over their bingo tickets or don't follow what's going on. Just a few weeks ago one of them sat completely still at a table all the time the numbers were being called. When the others left, he didn't get up, and when the cleaning lady finally tried to wake him up, she realised he was dead. Mum thought he might already have been dead the Tuesday before. I thought so too.

»Hello, Mr Fitzke,« I said, »I hope I didn't wake you up.«

Mr Fitzke looks even older than the pensioner who dropped dead at the bingo. And he's really stinky dirty. Apparently he doesn't have long to live either. That's why

---

whisk – Schneebesen

bumblebee – Hummel

he wears his pyjamas all the time, even when he goes to the supermarket. When he does drop dead, at least he'll be wearing the right clothes. Mr Fitzke once told Mrs Dahling he'd had a heart problem ever since he was very small. That's why he gets out of breath so easily, he said, and one day it'll be KA-POW! But even if he is about to die, he could still get dressed, or at least wash his pyjamas sometimes. At Christmas, for example. I wouldn't like to collapse in front of the cheese counter at the supermarket and smell totally gross, not when I'd only just died.

Mr Fitzke stared at me, so I thrust the piece of pasta under his nose. »Is this yours?«

»Where did you get that?«

»The pavement. Mrs Dahling thinks it could be rigatoni. The sauce is definitely Gorgonzola.«

»Was it just lying there,« he asked suspiciously, »or was it lying in something?«

»Huh?«

»Where's your brain gone? The piece of pasta, you dimwit!«

»What was the question again?«

Mr Fitzke rolled his eyes. Any minute now he would explode.

»For goodness' sake! Was your **bloody** piece of pasta just lying there on the pavement, or was it lying in something! Dog poo, for instance.«

---

bloody – in diesem Zusammenhang bedeutet es »verdammt«

»It was just lying there,« I said.

»Then let me take a closer look.«

He took the piece of pasta and turned it around in his fingers. Then he put it – my piece of pasta! – into his mouth and swallowed it. Without chewing.

And then he slammed the door. KER-ASH!

He's not right in the head!! The next piece of pasta I find, I'll drop it in dog poo, wiggle it round a bit, then bring it to Mr Fitzke, and when he asks if it was lying in something I'll tell him it's Bolognese sauce.

I'd really wanted to ask everybody who lived in the building about that piece of pasta, but now it was gone, swallowed up by Mr Fitzke. I was sad. It's always like that when you lose something. When I had it I didn't think it was that great, but now it was suddenly the best piece of pasta in the world. That was how it was with Mrs Dahling. Last winter she was moaning about her husband being a cheat, and now she's watching one romantic comedy after another and wishing he'd come back.

I wanted to go down to the second floor, but I thought it over and rang at the flat opposite Mr Fitzke's first. That was where the new person who had moved in two days ago lived. I hadn't seen him yet. I didn't have the piece of pasta any more, but it seemed like a good time to say hello. Maybe he'd let me in. I like visiting other people's flats.

This flat had been empty for a long time because it was so expensive. Mum had thought about renting it. There's more light on the fourth floor than on the second and even a bit of a view. You can look out through the trees over to the old, flat-roofed hospital on the other side of the road. But when Mum found out what the flat would cost, she had to drop the idea. Luckily for me, because then Mr Fitzke would have been right next door to us. The greedy pig.

The new person's name was Mr Westlake. That's what it said on the sign under the doorbell. He wasn't at home, and I was actually a little bit happy about that. It made me nervous, thinking that I'd have to say his name out loud. East and west, if you see what I mean. I always get left and right mixed up, even on the compass. When it's a matter of left or right, the lottery balls in my head always start to jumble.

I was angry as I ran down the stairs. If Mr Fitzke hadn't destroyed my **evidence**, it would have been a great day to be a detective. The pool of suspects was very small. For example, I could rule out the two fancy apartments on the fifth floor. The Runge-Blawetzkys had gone off on holiday the day before, and Mr Marrak, who lives next door to them, hadn't been seen for two whole days. He was probably staying at his girlfriend's, who also did his washing for him. Every few weeks Mr Marrak could be seen running around with a giant bag of washing. He ran out of the building, back into the building, back out, back in and on it went. Mrs Dahling once said that the young men of today were useless. Once upon a time they would just take a tooth-

evidence – Beweismittel

brush with them when they went out, and today they took half their wardrobe. Mr Marrak wasn't at home in any case. Yesterday's junk mail was still sticking out of his letterbox in the hall downstairs. If you watch murder mysteries instead of **smoochy** films, you start noticing things like that right away.

OK, that was the fifth floor crossed off. Mr Fitzke and the new man with the compass thing in his name live on the fourth floor. On the third floor, across from Mrs Dahling, lives Mr Kiesling. There's no point knocking on his door until the evening anyway because he's out at work during the day. He works as a dental technician in a laboratory.

On the floor below are Mum and I, and across from us the six Kesslers, two adults and four children, but they're on holiday too. The Kesslers own their flat and there's a staircase connecting their second-floor flat with their other flat on the floor below. Mr and Mrs Kessler need a lot of space with all those kids.

Most of all I had been looking forward to visiting the other flat on the first floor, the one below Mum and I. That's where Jule lives, along with Berts and Massoud. They're students. But I couldn't go and knock without the piece of pasta. Berts is all right. I can't stand Massoud because Jule likes him more than me. And that's all I'm saying on that subject for the moment. I should have started

---

smoochy – romantisch

my investigation down there, or at old Mr Mommsen's, the **caretaker** – he lives on the ground floor.

Ah well, never mind.

So it's back up to the second floor and home.

As I went into the flat, Mum was standing in the hall in front of the gold mirror with the little fat cherubs on it. She had pulled up her sky-blue T-shirt and was looking at her chest in a worried way. Who knows how long she'd been standing there. I could see her thoughtful face in the mirror.

A lot of people, especially men, stare at Mum in the street. Not because she runs around with her T-shirt pulled up, but because she looks fantastic. She always wears short tight skirts and low-cut tops. High-heeled, silver or gold strappy sandals. Her blonde hair loose, long and silky, and a whole bunch of ringing, jingling bracelets, chains and earrings. I like her fingernails best of all. They're really long. Mum glues something new onto them every week. Tiny, glittering fish or a small **ladybird** on each one, for example. She always says that there are plenty of men out there who are into that and that's why she does so well at work.

»Sooner or later the girls will start to droop,« Mum said to her reflection in the mirror, and to me. »Another two or three years and gravity will have its way. Life's all about crossing off the days.«

---

caretaker – Hausmeister

ladybird – Marienkäfer

I didn't know what gravity was. I would have to look it up. I always look up things I don't know in the dictionary, so that I get cleverer. Or sometimes I ask people. Mum or Mrs Dahling or my teacher, Mr Wehmeyer. I write down what I've discovered. Like this:

> GRAVITY: When something is heavier than something else, it pulls the other thing towards it. For example, the earth is heavier than almost everything else, that's why nothing falls off it. A man called Isaac Newton discovered gravity. It is dangerous for breasts and apples. And possibly for other round things too.

»And then?« I said.

»Then I'll get some new ones,« Mum said decisively. »We're talking about my floating **assets** here, after all.« She sighed, pulled down her T-shirt and turned towards to me. »How was school?«

»All right.«

She knows not to say anything about my special classes, because I hate talking about them. For years Mr Wehmeyer has been trying to sort out the lottery balls in my head. I've thought about suggesting that he should turn off the lottery

---

assets – Vermögen

machine before he starts messing around with the balls, but I never actually have. If he doesn't know that, that's his bad luck.

»Why did Mr Wehmeyer ask you to go in today?« said Mum. »I thought yesterday was the last day of school?«

»It was for a holiday project. Some writing.«

»You, writing?« She wrinkled up her forehead. »What are you writing?«

»Just something about me,« I murmured. It was more complicated than that, but I didn't want to let Mum in on it until I'd tried it out successfully.

»I see.« Her forehead smoothed out. »Have you had anything to eat?« She ran one hand through my hair, leaned over and kissed me on the forehead.

»Nah.«

»So you're hungry?«

»Yeah.«

»OK. I'll make us some **fish fingers**.« She disappeared into the kitchen. I tossed my rucksack through the open door into my bedroom, then followed her, sat at the dinner table and watched.

»I need to ask you something, Rico,« Mum said as she melted butter in the pan.

My head automatically slipped down between my shoulders. Whenever Mum asks me something and uses my name at the same time, that means she's been thinking about

---

fish fingers – Fischstäbchen

things, and when she's been thinking about things, it's usually something serious. And by serious I mean difficult. And by difficult I mean lottery balls.

»What?« I asked cautiously.

»It's about Mr 2000.«

I wished the fish fingers were already done. Even an idiot could tell where this conversation was going.

Mum opened the fridge, scraping and digging around in the freezer compartment with a knife to free the packet of fish fingers from its covering of blue ice. »He let another child go,« she continued. »One from Lichtenberg this time. That's the fifth already. The one before was from –«

»Wedding, I know.«

And the three before that were from Kreuzberg, Tempelhof and Charlottenburg. Mr 2000 has been keeping everybody in Berlin on the edge of their seats for three months. On television they said he was probably the most cunning child kidnapper of all time. Some people call him the ALDI kidnapper, after the supermarket, because his **ransoms** are so low. He lures little boys and girls into his car and drives off with them, and afterwards he writes their parents a letter: *Dear Parents, If you would like little Claudia back, it will cost you only 2000 euros. Think carefully before getting the police involved over such a ridiculously small sum, because if you do, your child will come back to you in pieces.*

---

ransom – Lösegeld

Up until now, none of the parents had involved the police until after they had paid up and their child popped up safe. But everybody in Berlin is waiting for the day when some little Claudia or Alexander or other doesn't come home in one piece because their parents have messed up. Some people might be quite happy that their child had been kidnapped and wouldn't cough up a penny. Or they might be really poor and only have fifty euros to their name. If you only gave Mr 2000 fifty euros, it's likely that the only piece left of your child would be a hand. The interesting question was which part he would send back, the hand or the rest of the body. My bet is on the hand. It would be less noticeable. And a giant **parcel** for everything-minus-the-hand would cost fifty euros in postage all by itself.

If you ask me, 2000 euros is a ton of money. But in an emergency, as Berts once explained to me, anybody can get their hands on cash if they put their minds to it. Berts is studying for an Em-Bee-Ay, which has something to do with money, so he must know what he's talking about.

»Do you have 2000 euros?« I asked Mum. You need to be prepared. In an emergency she could break into my **piggy bank**. You put the coins into the slit in the glass dome. I've had my piggy bank in the shape of the Reichstag for as long as I can remember and I'm pretty sure I must have saved

---

parcel – Paket

piggy bank – Sparschwein

enough for an arm or a leg. For twenty or thirty euros, Mum would at least have a small piece to remember me by.

»2000 euros,« she said. »Who do you think I am?«

»Would you be able to get that much money?«

»For you? Even if I had to kill for it, love.«

There was a crack and a thick piece of ice landed on the kitchen floor. Mum picked it up, made a noise like *pfff* or *hhmmph* and threw it into the sink. »This freezer really needs defrosting.«

»But I'm not as small as the other kids who were kidnapped. And I'm older.«

»Yeah, I know.« She prised the packet open. »But I should still have taken you to school every day for the last few weeks and picked you up again.«

Mum works until early in the morning. When she comes home, she brings me a fresh bread roll and gives me a kiss before I leave for school, and then she goes to bed. She usually doesn't get up until the afternoon, long after I'm back home again. She would never manage to take me to school and pick me up again.

She held her breath for a second and scratched her nose. »Am I a bad mother, Rico?«

»Course not!«

She looked at me thoughtfully for a moment; then tipped the deep-frozen fish fingers out of the packet and into the pan. The butter was so hot that it hissed. Mum took a quick step back. »Oh God! Now I stink of the stuff!«

She would shower anyway before going to work that

night. She always showers after fish fingers. It's the most expensive perfume in the world, she once said; nothing sticks to you like the smell of fish fingers. While they were **sizzling** in the pan, I told her about the piece of pasta I'd found and that Mr Fitzke had destroyed it, which was why I couldn't find out who it had belonged to.

»The old grouch,« she murmured.

Mum can't stand Mr Fitzke. A few years ago, when we had moved into Dieffe 93, she had dragged me through the entire building so that we could introduce ourselves to the neighbours. Her hand was very sweaty, and she held me really tightly. Mum is brave, but she still has feelings. She was afraid that people wouldn't like us when they found out she worked in a nightclub and I was a bit different. Mr Fitzke had answered her knock and stood there in his pyjamas. Unlike Mum, who kept a straight face, I grinned. That was my mistake. And then Mum said, Hello, I've just moved in, and this is my son Rico. He's a bit different, but it's not his fault. So if he ever gets up to anything …

Mr Fitzke **squinted** at us and **pulled a face** as though he had a bad taste in his mouth. Then, without saying a word, he slammed the door in our faces. Ever since then he's called me a dimwit.

»Did he call you a dimwit?« Mum asked.

---

sizzling – brutzeln

to squinted – hier: die Augen zusammenkneifen

pulling a face – ein Gesicht machen

»Nah.« There was no point getting her worked up.

»The old **grouch**,« she said again.

She didn't ask why I absolutely had to know who the piece of pasta belonged to. That was *just another one of Rico's ideas*. She was right. There was no point asking.

I watched her as she turned the fish fingers. She hummed a song and shifted her weight from the left foot to the right and back again. While the fish fingers were frying, she set the table. The sun fell through the window and there was the tasty smell of summer and fish in the air. I felt happy. I like it when Mum cooks or does one of those other **look-aftering** things that mums do.

»Blood sauce?« she said, when she was finished.

»Yep.«

She put the bottle of tomato ketchup on the table and pushed my plate towards me. »So I won't be taking you to school then?«

I shook my head. »It's the holidays now, anyway. Maybe they'll catch him before school starts again.«

»Are you sure?«

»Yeeesss!«

»Good.«

She was **shovelling** the fish fingers down her throat at top speed. »I have to go in a sec,« she said in reply to

---

grouch – Griesgram

look-aftering – sich um etwas kümmern

to shovel – schaufeln

my questioning look. »I'm going to the hairdresser's with Irina.« Irina is Mum's best friend. She works at the club too. »Strawberry blonde, what do you think?«

»Is that red?«

»No. It's blonde with a hint of red.«

»What's that got to do with strawberries?«

»They have a hint of it too.«

»Strawberries are bright red.«

»Only when they're ripe.«

»But before that they're green. And what sort of hint is it?«

»That's just what they call it.«

Mum doesn't like it when I keep on at her, and I don't like it when she talks and I don't understand what she's saying. Some things have really silly names, and you have to ask why they're called what they're called. I wonder, for example, why strawberries are called strawberries, even though they've got nothing to do with straw.

Mum pushed away her empty plate. »We still need a few things for the weekend. I could pick up the stuff myself, but …«

»I'll do it.«

»You're a love.« She grinned with relief, got up and hurriedly rummaged through her trouser pockets. »I've made a list, hang on a sec …«

Mum's trousers are so tight that I'm afraid I'll have to cut her out of them one of these days. I ask myself why she always stuffs everything into her trouser pockets. She's won at least ten plastic handbags at bingo, but she never uses them. She doesn't even keep them. She **auctions** them off on eBay.

»It's not much.« She held out the crumpled shopping list. »There's money in the drawer. The most important thing is the toothpaste. And butter's not on the list but there's none left. Will you remember, or should I –«

I speared the first fish finger with my fork and casually dunked it in the blood sauce. »I'll remember,« I said.

Hopefully.

---

to auction sth. off – etwas versteigern

SATURDAY AGAIN

OSKAR

The shopping went really well. Toothpaste, butter, pretzel sticks, salad stuff and yoghurt. I held out the money to the woman at the **till** in Edeka and she gave me my change and said to say hello to my mum. The way she said it, she looked as though she actually wished Mum a really painful death. After we had moved in at Dieffe, Mum went in to see her to explain politely that I can't do **sums** and that she had broken both the arms of the last person who'd tried to cheat me.

I went out of the shop. There was a light wind moving the leaves on the trees in the street – I've forgotten what the trees are called, or I never knew in the first place, but they look great. The bark on their trunks peels off like **varnish** on an old door and underneath you can see lighter bark that's also peeling off, and more underneath that. You wonder where trees stop on the inside.

Sunlight shone down on millions of leaves and threw tiny shadows onto the pavements. There were people everywhere, lots of them sitting outside on the pavement in front of pubs and restaurants, and music from the open windows of the blocks of flats made its way down to the pavements. I was very happy at that moment. I felt good about myself.

Dieffe is very long and has everything you need. The Edeka and a **late-night corner shop**, two fruit and veg-

---

till – Kasse

sums – Rechnen

varnish – Lack

late-night corner shop – Spätkauf, Kiosk

etable shops, an **off-licence**, a baker's, butcher's – those kinds of places. You don't have to turn off anywhere, and that's why Mum picked such a long, straight street for me to live on: because I don't remember the way very well if it has corners. Mum says my sense of direction is like a drunken pigeon in a windy snowstorm. But from Dieffe I can actually go to school by myself. All I have to do is go out of the house, walk a little way to the **chemist's** on the corner and then turn off upwards, in the direction of the Landwehrkanal. From then on I keep going straight, across the Admiralsbrücke to school. The street carries on after the school, through Little Istanbul towards Kottie, but I've never been brave enough to go any further than the Doyum kebab house, just *before* Kottie.

I wondered if I should look for another piece of pasta on the way home. Maybe it hadn't flown out of the window at Dieffe 93, but a passer-by had lost it or dropped it on purpose instead.

> PASSER-BY: **Pedestrian.** Had to ask Mum what we call them again. It's bad enough translating foreign words into words you understand. The other way around is even harder.

off-licence – Spirituosengeschäft

chemist's – Apotheke

pedestrian – Passant

I shuffled along and thought about Hansel and Gretel, who laid a trail of breadcrumbs in the forest so they wouldn't get lost. Maybe somebody in the area had laid a trail of pasta pieces. If they did, then they are even more of a child proddity than I am. They'll never find their way back when there are greedy pigs like Mr Fitzke around. Hansel and Gretel had their trail of crumbs eaten up by the birds of the forest, and where did the two of them end up? That's right, with the big bad wolf!

I stopped at the playground. The playground is framed by Grimmstraße; it loops around up by the canal and comes back down to meet Dieffe – so it's kind of a double street. The playground is large and always full of mums and toddlers when the weather is good. In Neukölln, where we lived before we moved here, Mum often went to the playground with me. I had a **spade** and a sieve and all kinds of sand buckets to play with, until I dug a hole and threw them in it. I covered them all up with my hands and never found any of them again.

I looked at the playground a little longer and smiled for a bit at the little **squiddlers**, who were all much smarter than me, and then I remembered the piece of pasta. I walked slowly over the pavement, looking at the grey cobblestones. I saw a scrunched-up chocolate wrapper, a few pieces of

---

spade – Schaufel

squiddlers – Knirpse, kleine Kinder

glass lying on the floor in front of the big recycling containers and an old cigarette butt. Then I saw small feet wearing brightly coloured socks in open sandals.

I raised my head. The boy who was standing there in front of me only came up as far as my chest. That is to say, his dark-blue crash helmet only came up as far as my chest. It was the kind of crash helmet that motorcycle riders wear. I didn't know you could get them in children's sizes too. He looked like he had a screw loose. The see-through thing on his helmet was pushed up.

> VISOR: A see-through thing. I asked Berts about it because he rides a motorbike. He told me that Jule and Massoud had gone on holiday together. Hmph ...

»What are you doing?« the boy said. His teeth were enormous. They looked as though he could tear entire pieces out of large animals with them: horses or giraffes or animals of that sort.

»I'm looking for something.«

»If you tell me what it is, I can help you.«

»A piece of pasta.«

He searched the pavement. As he lowered his head, a beam of sunlight struck his helmet and bounced off it. I noticed a tiny, bright-red toy aeroplane fastened to his short-sleeved shirt with a safety pin, like a **badge**. One of the aeroplane's wings had broken off. The small boy also looked in the bushes in front of the playground fence; I hadn't thought of that.

»What kind of pasta is it?« he said.

»Definitely a lost piece. Rigatoni, but I'm not sure. I won't know that until I find it, otherwise it wouldn't be lost.«

»Hm …« He put his head on one side. The mouth with the large teeth opened wide. »Are you not quite right in the head?«

Well, thanks a lot!

»I'm a child proddity.«

»Is that a fact?« Now he looked really interested. »I'm a child prodigy.«

Now I was interested, too. Even though the boy was much smaller than I was, he suddenly felt much bigger. It was a strange feeling. We looked at each other for such a long time that I thought we would still be standing there when the sun went down. I had never seen a child prodigy, apart from on TV in one of those talent contests. There was a girl who had played something really difficult on the violin and at the same time the host of the show called out numbers a mile long and she had to say if they were **prime numbers** or not. Mrs Dahling swallowed down a canapé in

---

badge – Abzeichen

prime number – Primzahl

one go and said that the little girl would go far in life, which is why I thought prime numbers were something important. Turns out they're not.

> PRIME NUMBER: A prime number is a number that you can only divide by the number 1 and by itself if you want to avoid fractures. Broken arms, for example. If I had been that TV presenter, I would have asked the girl why she didn't play the flute or the trumpet instead of the violin. That way, if you fracture your arm, you can keep on blowing.

»I've got to go now,« I said to the boy finally. »Before it gets dark. Otherwise I might get lost.«

»Where do you live?«

»Over there, in the yellow building. No. 93. On the right.«

I could have kicked myself as soon as I said on the right. First of all, I didn't really know if it was on the right – it might have been on the left. Secondly, the old hospital is across from the row of blocks of flats, stretched out like a sleeping cat, and you can tell right away that that isn't a building where people live.

The boy followed my outstretched arm. When he saw number 93, he wrinkled up his forehead as though he had just made an amazing discovery and then wrinkled it down again as though he was **thinking deeply about something**.

Finally, his forehead smoothed out and he grinned. »You're really not all there, are you? If something is right in front of you and all you've got to do is keep going straight, you can't possibly get lost.«

At least I'd got the right side of the street. I was getting just a little angry anyway. »Oh yeah? Well, I can. And if you are really as clever as you say you are, you would know that there are people who can.«

»I –«

»And another thing. It's not one bit funny!«

All the lottery balls had turned red and were clacking against each other. »It's not my fault that sometimes things go missing from my brain! I don't mean to be stupid. I'm not stupid because I'm lazy!«

»Hey, I –«

»I bet you're one of those superbrains who knows everything and always has to show off about something because otherwise nobody is interested in them unless they play the violin on telly!«

It's very embarrassing, but when I get really worked up about something, when something isn't fair, for example, I start to cry. There's absolutely nothing I can do about it. The boy looked shocked under his crash helmet.

»Don't cry! I didn't mean to –«

---

thinking deeply about something – intensiv über etwas nachdenken

»And I know what a prime number is!« I shouted.

I was upset – that was about the only thing I did know at that moment. The boy didn't say anything else. He looked down at his sandals. Then he looked up again. He stretched out his hand. It was so small that both of his would have fitted into one of mine.

»I'm Oskar,« he said. »And I would like to apologise **sincerely**. I shouldn't have made fun of you. It was arrogant.«

I had no idea what he meant by the last word, but I understood he was sorry.

ARROGANT: When somebody looks down on somebody else. So Oskar can't be all that clever because at the end of the day he's a lot smaller than I am and has to keep looking up at me.

You have to be nice when somebody apologises. If somebody is just pretending, you can keep on being mad, but Oskar meant it sincerely. He'd said so himself.

»I'm Rico,« I said and shook his hand. »My dad was Italian.«

»Is he dead?«

»Of course. Otherwise I wouldn't have said he was.« My teacher, Mr Wehmeyer, told me that one of the strengths in

---

sincerely – aufrichtig

my writing were the tenses: the past, present and future, and the If-I-were-you tense.

»I'm sorry. How did he die?«

I didn't answer. I've never told anybody how my dad died. It's nobody's business. It's a very sad story. I **wrinkled my nose**, looked over the fence at the playground and tried to think of something else. For example, whether there were spades and buckets and sieves buried there too, and if so, how many and which colours. There were probably hundreds. If I dug them up, Mum could auction them off on eBay with her handbags.

Oskar wasn't sure what to do when he realised I wasn't going to say anything else. At some point he nodded his head and said, »I have to go home now«.

»Me too. Otherwise the butter will melt.« I lifted up the shopping bag. And then, because he looked so **neat and tidy** in his funny clothes, like one of those kids who have to eat fruit and vegetables and sugar-free muesli from the health food shop, I said, »We ran out of butter because we had fish fingers with blood sauce for lunch today.«

I went and decided not to turn around. I didn't want to give him the impression that I thought he was great with his crash helmet and his monster teeth. But then I did turn around after all and I saw him disappearing down Dieffe in

---

to wrinkle the nose – die Nase rümpfen

neat and tidy – sauber und aufgeräumt

the other direction. From a distance he looked like a very small child with a very large blue head.

It was only when I was back at home and I'd put the butter in the fridge and begun to scratch the ice out of the **freezer compartment** that I realised I hadn't asked Oskar what he was doing all by himself on our block. Or why he had a small, bright red aeroplane on his shirt. Or why he was wearing a motorbike crash helmet, even though he was on foot.

Mrs Dahling's curls had turned out very nicely. I gave her the pretzel sticks as she let me in. The evening light was all red-golden and fell into the hallway through the open door of the living room. There were little pictures in plastic frames all over the walls; most of them **contained** drawings of small children with very large eyes who were standing in different places – in front of the Eiffel Tower or on a bridge in Venice, for example. There were pictures with clowns too and other things. Half of the children were crying.

»I'm not doing too well, my dear,« said Mrs Dahling and closed the door to the flat. »I'm having one of my grey days.«

---

freezer compartment – Gefrierfach

to contain – beinhalten

I almost cheered. A grey day meant that we wouldn't be watching a romantic film. I've got nothing against them, but they make me a little nervous. There are no romantic films about proddities – it's as though nobody loves people like me. OK, there's *Forrest Gump*, but that film doesn't have a happy ending, and I can't stand Forrest anyway. He's so **pushy** and greedy.

Mrs Dahling placed a hand on my shoulder and guided me into her living room. I'm not so stupid that I would lose my way in her little flat, but I didn't say anything. Her grey days aren't easy and you have to be a bit nice to her.

»Did you find out who the piece of pasta belonged to? Was it Mr Fitzke?«

»Nah.«

I didn't tell her that the stupid idiot had gobbled it up. I planted myself on the sofa and glanced at the table. There was a plate on it full of liver paté canapés, mini-cucumbers and tomato halves. My stomach started rumbling. Mrs Dahling made the best canapés in the world.

»If it wasn't Mr Fitzke,« she thought out loud, »then it was probably one of those Kessler brats.«

»Nah. The Kesslers are on holiday. They went yesterday. Just like the Runge-Blawetzkys.«

The Kesslers have been on telly and in the paper and everything. They're a sensation because Mrs Kessler had two sets of twins in the same year, two boys in January,

---

pushy – aufdringlich

two girls in December. They just about manage to fit in Christmas and New Year between the two sets of birthdays. Expensive piece of work, Mr Kessler always says, but with a proud grin. Two sets of twins, he'd like to see anyone compete with that. The twins are six and seven years old. Mrs Dahling **can't stand them**. She calls them the buy-one-get-one-free kids.

She put the pretzel sticks into a glass and placed it on the table next to the canapés. She turned the television on. We always watch the news before we start on the films: first the local evening news from Berlin, then the national news. Mrs Dahling is crazy about one of the newsreaders on the local news. He's got brown eyes like a teddy bear, and he's called Ulf Brauscher and Mrs Dahling thinks he's fantastic. The last time she came round for a drop of whisky with Mum, she said she thought he was gorgeous.

Today Ulf Brauscher's beautiful brown eyes looked very serious because the evening news was about Mr 2000 and the child from Lichtenberg who had been set free. The parents didn't want to give any interviews, so the news was showing photos of the other children, pictures every Berliner knew from the newspaper and the **telly**: two boys and two girls, none of them older than seven. All of them were smiling in their photos, apart from little Sophia. Her photo was slightly blurry, but you could still see how close together her eyes

---

can't stand them – kann sie nicht ausstehen

telly – Glotze

were in her flat moon face. Her lips were narrow and almost as pale as her thin eyebrows, her stringy, blonde hair hung down over her shoulders and she was wearing a wrinkled, dark-pink T shirt with a thick red splat of strawberry jam or something like that on it. She looked like someone who would get laughed at or teased in the school playground. Sophia was Mr 2000's second victim and I felt more sorry for her than for anybody else. I know what it's like when other people are always making fun of you for being different.

Ulf Brauscher explained that there was still no sign of the kidnapper and then the news moved on to politics. Next to me, Mrs Dahling made a **snorting noise**.

»I wish I had that man's address.«

»Ulf Brauscher's?« I could remember his name because it flashed up on the screen regularly. Otherwise my memory for names was down the **plughole**.

»No, the address of the kidnapper.« Mrs Dahling pushed half a tomato into her mouth. »There are times when I'd like to send him a personal invitation to come and collect those Kessler kids. Nobody'd miss 'em if you ask me.«

She snorted again. »Those buy-one-get-one-free kids are the worst things to have ever lived in this building!«.«

Mrs Dahling pushed a mini-cucumber down after her half tomato. She made little crunches as she chewed on it. Then she licked her fingers.

---

snorting noise – schnaubendes Geräusch

plughole – Abfluss

»I think Mr Fitzke is worse.«

She waved away the thought and fished out a few pretzel sticks.

»Nah, he's just putting it on. Another canapé, Rico?«

> PUTTING IT ON: Pretending. You'd think you could use one simple word in the first place instead of three confusing ones.

I took a canapé and a piece of cucumber. Mrs Dahling chewed her pretzel sticks, then suddenly she grabbed the remote control and turned down the sound on the television. They were showing pictures of the cathedral and a couple of cranes, but I couldn't hear what was going on. Quiet spread through the living room. Mrs Dahling looked **straight ahead** with slightly teary eyes and didn't move again. I looked at her out of the corner of my eye, chewing my canapé and cucumber carefully. It's always a bit creepy when she has one of her grey days.

»What?« said Mrs Dahling after a while, reluctantly, without turning her head in my direction.

»Perhaps you should go out sometimes,« I said.

»Is that your idea or your mother's?«

»Mine.«

---

straight ahead – geradeaus

It was Mum's idea. But I'm not so **daft** that I don't know why people have grey days. You have to be careful as a child proddity not to say things you haven't thought up yourself. Otherwise, just like that, people start thinking you're a liar and actually quite clever after all and then they start giving you sums to do and other stuff. Anyway, you get grey days because you're lonely, and you won't meet other people unless you go out or find somebody on the internet. I've got no idea how old Mrs Dahling is, almost certainly nearly fifty. But there has to be somebody out there who likes eating canapés too. In any case, no man has turned up at the Karstadt butcher's counter for her yet.

The local news was over. Ulf Brauscher disappeared. Mrs Dahling pressed the button on the remote control firmly. The screen went black, then the pink logo of the DVD player appeared.

»We're watching a murder mystery,« said Mrs Dahling as she pushed herself up from the sofa and went over to the **cupboard** with the film collection. »Miss Marple.«

This time I did cheer out loud.

---

daft – bescheuert

cupboard – Schrank

Later, when I was back home, lying in bed, I couldn't fall asleep. Part of it was Miss Marple's fault. I always get really nervous when I watch one of her murder mysteries because I'm afraid that something will happen to her. I get so worked up that I always forget I've seen the film before and that she survived every other time.

Part of the problem was that there was a full moon. It **lit up** the dark, dull windows of the empty flats in the building behind ours. Old curtains were still hanging in many of them. It's just my luck that it's the third floor that I can see especially well from my bed. That's where Miss Bonhöfer killed herself. Miss Bonhöfer was an old lady. One day she got lung cancer and didn't fancy going to hospital. She turned on the gas, lit a final cigarette and waited a while. Then KA-BOOM!

First of all they thought the building hadn't been damaged all that much by the explosion. The flats where everything was smashed got new windows and stuff, but when they looked at the stairway, they realised the explosion had left cracks in the walls of the fourth and fifth floors. The whole place was in danger of collapse and everybody who lived there had to move out.

The windows in the stairway were boarded up, the door in the yard that led to the apartment building got a big new security lock, and since then the various owners of the flats have been fighting over who should pay to have it rebuilt.

---

to light up – erleuchten

That was years and years ago. But Miss Bonhöfer has been haunting her old rooms since then. That's what the caretaker, Mr Mommsen, told me right after we moved in. He had just started his job when Miss Bonhöfer killed herself. He firmly believes that her ghost is still looking for an **ashtray** or something else in her old flat.

Something makes me look over there, whether I want to or not. I've often thought of asking Mum to put up curtains or a blind, but then she might think I was a softy. Sometimes I think I can see even more shadowy shadows behind the shadows in Miss Bonhöfer's flat, **flitting** through the empty rooms. I know I'm just imagining the shadowier shadows, but that doesn't make it easier. Especially when you really have to go to the toilet but aren't brave enough to get up – and I've never been brave enough when Mum is at work at night and I'm alone in the flat. I haven't wet the bed for a long time, but if I watch the shadowier shadows flitting around for longer than a minute I just might. That's why I usually pull the blanket over my head before going to sleep.

Just like today.

Under the blanket I thought about Oskar and whether I would ever see him again. Then I fell asleep.

---

ashtray – Aschenbecher

to flit – flitzen

SUNDAY

THE HOLIDAY DIARY

I've taken most of Sunday to write down Saturday. But that's OK; I had nothing else to do because Mum was asleep all day. She stays at the club longer than usual at the weekend. She didn't come home until ten in the morning and fell into bed right away. Which is why she didn't notice that I was sitting at the computer all day. If my experiment goes wrong, then at least she won't be disappointed.

All this writing was Wehmeyer's idea. That was the reason I had to go and see him on Saturday, even though it was already the holidays. It started with a story about the Landwehrkanal that I wrote two weeks ago. It really made an impression on Mr Wehmeyer, and he wanted to talk to me about it.

»Your spelling is **hair-raising**, Rico,« he said. »But there's something about *the way* you write. You're a good story-teller ... leaving aside the **digressions**. You know: the part about the North Sea.«

The canal flows almost right behind Dieffe 93. You can sit very comfortably on the bank under the lovely **weeping willows** or on the grass in between all the other people. You can look out over the shining water or tease the paddling swans. Now and then a boat with tourists passes by and you can wave at them. They wave back very excitedly as though

---

hair-raising – haarsträubend

digressions - Abschweifungen

weeping willow – Trauerweide

they've never seen a boy sitting on a canal bank before. It's all in the story.

The digression part that Mr Wehmeyer mentioned was my favourite bit, the bit where I imagined how it would feel to be a dead body floating in a canal. Imagine it's winter and you've just broken through the ice. The current carries you under the blue-black ice from the Landwehrkanal into the River Spree. I looked at the map of Germany to see where you would go from there: the Spree flows into the River Havel and the Havel flows into the River Elbe and the Elbe flows into the North Sea and the North Sea belongs to the Atlantic. So if you drown in the canal, it's really quite a trip. You get to go on a fantastic journey down three rivers and finally into the ocean, unless, of course, you get caught in a ship's propeller and get totally **scrunched**, which would be annoying.

Mr Wehmeyer had a strange look on his face. »Are you worried about Mr 2000? Does it frighten you, all this stuff with the kidnappings?«

So it *was* about the scrunched-up dead body. I shook my head. I had been thinking about somebody else while I was writing, not about the kidnapper, but that was none of Mr Wehmeyer's business.

He nodded and looked at the wall with all the photos of his kids and his wife and his dog and his motorbike, which is nowhere near as nice as Berts'.

---

to scrunch – hier: zerstückeln

»I've been thinking,« he said. »What would you say to keeping a **diary**? About the things you get up to in the holidays? The things you think about, the things you do … Are you and your mum going on holiday?«

»No. Is this homework?«

»Let's put it like this. If you give it a good go, I'll give you less homework after the holidays.«

That sounded good.

»How much am I supposed to write?«

»Let's say … I'll be happy with ten pages. If you manage twenty, I'll throw in a bonus.«

»What's that?«

»An extra reward.«

That sounded even better. Even so, I was a bit nervous. Twenty pages is a lot.

»And the spelling mistakes?« I asked suspiciously.

»Don't worry about that. Don't you have a computer at home?«

»Mum's got one. From eBay.«

Mum not only gets rid of her plastic handbags from bingo on eBay, she also buys cheap stuff there, like clothes.

»Does the computer have a **word-processing programme** with an autocorrect function?«

»What does autocorrect mean?«

»It's like a built-in teacher.«

---

diary – Tagebuch

word-processing programme – Textverarbeitungsprogramm

BUILT-IN TEACHER FUNCTION: Now and again somebody explains a word and then you're even more confused. In the beginning anyway. With autocorrect, for example, you might well be asking yourself how a teacher can possibly live inside a computer.

Sometimes Mr Wehmeyer puts together extra long words and sentences just to annoy us. If I'm having a bad day, I get worked up and then the lottery machine starts up. But today I wasn't going to get annoyed. It was the holidays. And besides, I was quite excited by his idea. A diary …

It took a while, but then I sorted out all his words and understood them. When Mum bought our computer, a word-processing programme and a lot of other stuff came with it for free. Mum uses it now and then to write letters. I nodded.

»Good,« said Mr Wehmeyer. »Because a programme like that corrects your spelling mistakes automatically.«

I was astounded. »Really?«

»Really. But do me a favour and at least look at some of the worst mistakes. Maybe you'll learn something.«

Was he off his rocker? If I looked at each mistake one by one, the lottery balls would go crazy.

»Deal?« said Mr Wehmeyer.

»Deal.«

He grinned and raised his hand. »Give me five.«

I pushed my chair back, stood up, quickly said goodbye and left. If he was about to move on to maths, that would spoil everything.

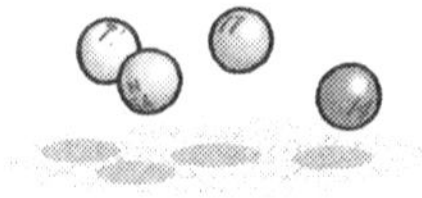

Well, that's it up until now. And I've written more than twenty pages. So I can take a break. Writing is hard work. But I'll get my bonus. Mr Wehmeyer will be amazed.

The automatic correction thing isn't all that great, though. A few pages back I'd written a word the wrong way, *swones* instead of *swans*. The programme suggested the following sentence: *You can look out over the shining water or tease the paddling* **scones**.

---

scones – Scones, Teegebäck

MONDAY

THE NEW NEIGHBOUR

Around lunchtime there was a knock at the front door. Mum had just got up and shuffled past my room. I heard her **pottering about** in the kitchen, making coffee.

»Can you answer?« she called.

I had never seen the man at the door before. He was tall and thin, with short black hair, electric-blue eyes and a small scar on his chin. He looked like an actor.

»Hello!« He smiled and stretched out his hand. »I thought it was time I came by and introduced myself. I moved in a few days ago, upstairs on the fourth floor. I'm Simon Westlake.«

I didn't answer. I stared at the scar on his chin and his outstretched hand then back at his chin again and wished he was just called Mr Lake. A small needle on a compass was spinning crazily in front of my eyes – west, east, west, east. I went red and began to sweat. That's the problem with the lottery balls: they start to roll around whether it suits me or not. I could hear them clacking against the inside of my skull.

Mr Lake was still wearing a friendly smile, but there were suddenly two tiny question marks in his eyes, as though he'd never seen a boy sweating so badly before. His hand was still hanging in the air in front of me. He must have thought I was crazy. I thought I'd better pull myself together. A name with a single compass point in it shouldn't be that difficult, even for a child proddity like me.

---

to potter about – herumwirtschaften

»Who is it?« Mum called from the kitchen.

»Mr Eastlake,« I yelled back. »The new neighbour from the fourth floor.«

Clack, clack, clacker-dee-clack.

»I can always come back ...« Mr Lake began, and then his voice **seeped away** like the rain in one of our **gutters**. He looked over my shoulder with wide eyes. I turned around.

Mum had come into the hallway in her bare feet. She was fiddling around with her freshly dyed strawberry-blonde hair, trying to tie it into a ponytail at the neck. I like it when she's sleepy. She looks like a little girl. She looked very pretty, but I would have preferred it if she'd been wearing more than a man's shirt to come to the door – it was so short you could see her knickers!

Mr Lake looked her up and down very quickly without moving his head. His cheeks started to go red. If he begins to sweat now too, we'll **be quits**, I thought.

»Just a second,« Mum said, as though he was only the postman, and slipped into the bathroom. There was a splashing of water. You could hear her gargling.

»She's using mouthwash,« I whispered to Mr Lake.

He nodded in a friendly way and pretended to be looking around our beautiful hallway, but he kept glancing at me strangely. Seconds later Mum came out of the bathroom in

---

to seep away – versickern

gutter – Regenrinne

to be quits – mit jdm. quitt sein

her Japanese dressing gown with the painted symbols on it. We sometimes guess at what they might mean – *Good Morning*, maybe, or *Peace on Earth* or *Eat More Vegetables!*

»Sorry,« she murmured. Then she was standing in front of Mr Lake before finally grabbing his outstretched hand. »Tanja Doretti.« She smiled. »At least I think so. I'm not quite awake yet.«

»Simon Westlake. I hope I haven't –«

»Not at all. Come on in.« She turned around and headed towards the kitchen. »Coffee?« she asked over her shoulder. »I've just put the machine on. I'm not much use before I've had my first cup.«

I once watched a film with Mrs Dahling about a famous Greek hero … His name began with O and he was in a wooden horse in a war and then he sailed round and about on his ship for years to get back to his wife. She'd stayed at home, where she was being chased by a thousand men who all fancied her loads. O clearly didn't know this, otherwise he might have got a bit more of a move on. Instead he kept getting lost in his boat and had all these crazy adventures, but in the end he finally got back to his wife and got rid of all the other blokes with bows and arrows etc. What a cool story!

Anyway, at some point during one of the journeys when he got lost, in the middle of a storm out at sea, O sailed past an island, and there were singing ladies there, some kind of mermaids. Anybody who heard them went completely mad and tried to reach them; and a few of O's men jumped into the water and drowned nastily. One of the sailors said their voices were like honey and milk, even though Mrs Dahling didn't think their **warbling** was all that great, more like **vinegar** with a lot of sugar in it. She almost turned over to watch *Musikantenstadl*, but she really wanted to know what would happen to O's wife. Anyway, O got his companions to tie him to the mast and that's how he escaped with his life.

Nobody had tied up Mr Lake. He followed Mum into the kitchen as though she'd just sung him a beautiful song, and he looked almost exactly as **delighted** as O had been tied to the ship's mast. Mum pointed to a chair and placed two cups on the table without saying a word. The coffee machine bubbled away. I sat down across from Mr Lake. He looked much more handsome than the actor who'd played O. And he looked really at home in our kitchen.

»Are you married?« I said.

He started to grin and shook his head. His teeth were very clean and white.

»Have you got a girlfriend?«

»Rico!« hissed Mum.

»Don't worry,« Mr Lake grinned, without shifting his gaze from me. He didn't answer the question, but I liked him anyway. I like Mr Kiesling from the third floor as

---

to warble – trillern, trällern

vinegar – Essig

delighted – erfreut, begeistert

well, or at least the way he looks. But he's normally pretty grumpy. He probably doesn't like children all that much. And Mr Kiesling would never marry Mum; he's not all that **keen on** women.

»We're going to bingo tomorrow night,« I said. »At the *Grey Bumblebees*. Do you want to come?«

»Rico, go to your room,« Mum ordered. »Please!«

»Bingo?« Mr Lake said. »I've never ... isn't that for pensioners?«

»Yes, but there's a spare place because one of them has just died. Except nobody noticed. And Mum almost always wins, sometimes even with my card!«

Even the lamest pensioner can cross off the numbers on their card faster than I can. But it's good fun all the same.

»Frederico!« Mum said in a **stern voice**. »Off with you!«

It's always serious when she uses my full name. I wondered what the matter was. It was just getting interesting between her and Mr Lake – the two of them about to have coffee together, etc. Who knows what they would talk about and knowing Mum she'd probably say completely the wrong thing. I could have helped her because I know from Mrs Dahling's romantic films exactly what you're supposed to say so that it all works out, but I couldn't do anything from my room. So I would miss the whole thing, unless, of course –

---

keen on – scharf auf

stern voice – strenge Stimme

»And if you listen in, I'll auction you off on eBay! I want to hear your door close behind you.«

Mum finally poured Mr Lake some coffee. Mr Lake looked at me, raised both his hands, shrugged his shoulders and **pulled a funny face**. No help to be had from him, then. He probably really wanted to be left alone with Mum.

Honestly!

I ran to my room really fast and banged my door shut behind me. Mum can't stand it when I do that, but she had nobody to blame but herself. Ten minutes later I heard Mr Lake saying goodbye in the hallway. I crept to the door and listened. He said thank you for the coffee and all that, but nothing along the lines of see you tomorrow evening at bingo.

Oh well!

The front door opened and closed. I shot straight out into the hallway, past Mum, who isn't used to me being so speedy. I really wanted to say goodbye to Mr Lake. Surely that was allowed. So I opened the door, rushed out into the stairway and –

It was probably the biggest collision Dieffe 93 has ever seen. What a mess! In front of our door three men had run into one another, and because I had Mr Lake on the brain, it took me a few seconds to notice the other two. One of them was Mr Marrak, who was trying to get up the stairs with all of today's and yesterday's post, or at least half of it,

---

to pull a funny face – ein lustiges Gesicht machen

because the rest was **scattered** across the floor. The other one was Mr Kiesling, who was trying to get down the stairs. At the very moment Mr Lake had walked out of our door, the other two must have met on the landing and now all three were tangled up in a big knot. There was a jangling and a clattering while Mr Marrak tried to collect his letters. He has his own security business, so he always carries a big bunch of keys on the belt of his red uniform, which has a small, golden safe **embroidered** on to it. Very fancy.

Mr Kiesling placed his hand over his chest and stared wide-eyed at Lake as though he wanted to **snog** him on the spot – perhaps he was thinking of tearing his shirt off. Mr Lake turned helplessly in one direction and then the other, and all of them were muttering: sorry, I wasn't looking, never mind, it's not a big deal, I was in such a rush, but nothing serious happened – who does that child belong to?

Something small had almost got lost in the general chaos. It looked all three men up and down, through a visor. Then it called out in horror: »If I hadn't had my helmet on, I'd be dead by now!«

---

to scatter – verstreuen

to embroider – besticken

to snog – knutschen

Mum was quite **gobsmacked** that somebody had come to visit me. She's always complaining that I don't have any friends. Now I had one. Admittedly, he was a bit small and probably also quite young, but Mum didn't seem all that bothered. She was much more interested in Oskar's blue motorcycle helmet.

»Since when do people wear something like that to ride a bicycle?« she said.

She was leaning against the kitchen stove, sipping from the coffee cup she held in her hands. Mr Lake's cup was standing all by itself between Oskar and me on the table, only half empty.

»I haven't got a bicycle,« Oskar said. His voice sounded muffled, because the visor on his helmet was still pushed down.

»I bet you don't have a motorbike either.«

Oskar looked at her as though she wasn't quite right in the head. But he did push up his visor. You still couldn't see his mouth properly, just the top row of his large white teeth.

»It's dangerous without a helmet,« he explained, as though Mum was the child and he the adult. »Accidents happen all the time.«

»Not in my kitchen they don't, young man!« Mum sounded almost insulted. »I'm sure Rico will confirm that for you.«

I wrinkled my forehead. »I did bang my head on the fridge last week.«

---

gobsmacked – erstaunt

»That wasn't an accident,« Mum said firmly. »You came out of the hall too fast and ran into the open door.«

Oskar didn't feel comfortable with Mum there, I could tell. He peered out from under his helmet like a **tortoise**. He was wearing a different shirt today, but the bright red aeroplane with the broken wing was pinned just above his heart. His little fingers were tapping on the table nervously, *rap tee-tap*. Oskar was probably afraid that Mum would think he was rude and demand that he take off his helmet.

He wasn't completely wrong about that, but not completely right either. Mum can deal with strange people. Her first rule is, never put pressure on anyone if they don't want to do something. At least not with words. But she looks. She looks at people for so long that they can't take it anymore and finally they give in.

She was looking at Oskar the way a scientist would look at a completely new type of plant he'd just discovered. I was wondering myself what Oskar looked like under his helmet. Maybe he wasn't actually afraid of accidents. Maybe he had two funny ears and was ashamed of them. Or no ears at all – like one of Mr 2000's **victims** who hadn't raised enough ransom money.

Oskar's fingers got slower and slower, and then they stopped their tapping. He raised his head, looked Mum

---

tortoise – Landschildkröte

victim – Opfer

right in the eyes and said »You can stare at me as long as you like. I don't care. But I'll stare back.«

And that's what he did. For the first time I noticed how green his eyes were. They really gleamed. Not nastily or angrily. They were gleaming because Oskar enjoyed staring back. At that moment I was really jealous of him for being a child prodigy. Whenever Mum stares at me, I always look straight at the floor, as though something really interesting is going on down there, like colourful ants running around or a fire on the carpet. Till I saw Oskar I'd never thought of staring back.

I wondered which one of them would win. Mum was my mum so I probably should have taken her side. She was good at staring and didn't bat an eyelid. But Oskar was only little, and I thought the whole staring contest was a bit unfair. Either Mum thought so too or she lost interest.

Whichever it was, she suddenly said: »I need new toenails.«

Oskar and I both looked at her toenails. There was a tiny dolphin on each one; the two little toes were the only places they hadn't fitted.

»What do you want to put on them instead?« Oskar said. It sounded like a peace offering.

Mum shrugged. »Not sure. Maybe some other kind of fish.«

She put her coffee cup down on the sink, pulled her Japanese dressing gown around her and went out of the kitchen.

Oskar waited until she was out of **earshot**, then he said quietly in my direction: »Dolphins aren't fish.«

»She likes you,« I said.

He shook his head. »She doesn't know if she likes me yet. She thinks I'm funny because of the helmet.« He pulled the visor back down. His voice sounded muffled again. »Every year almost forty thousand children die in accidents in Germany. Almost a third of them are passengers in cars. Almost forty per cent are on bikes. And twenty-five percent are pedestrians.«

Maths! I've already told you that it's not my strong point.

»Most of them are cut down on their way to school or while playing in the afternoon,« Oskar murmured darkly. »Most of the cyclists are killed because they're using the wrong lane. Most of the pedestrians because they run across the street without looking. I always look. Always!«

I realised that one of the big differences between Oskar and me is that I am in a good mood nearly all the time, but I don't know very much about anything, whereas Oskar knows all kinds of strange things, but he always expects the worst. That's probably what happens when you're very clever – you can't just think of nice things, you have to think of terrible things too.

I jumped up. I'd had an idea. »I'll show you something,« I said. »It's not dangerous at all and it's great!«

»What is it?«

---

earshot – Hörweite

»Wait, I have to ask Mum something first.«

I burst into the living room – today really was a fast day! Mum was curled up on our thinking chair in front of the **windowsill**. She was looking out of the window. She was miles away. There wasn't a trace of nail polish or new stickers for her toes. She'd probably lied and just wanted some peace and quiet.

»What do you think of him?« I whispered.

She turned to me and wrinkled her nose. »I think he's a bit odd. Where did you dig him up? I've never seen a kid with a crash helmet …«

»I don't mean Oskar. I mean Mr Lake.«

»Oh …« Suddenly she looked really tired, as though she hadn't slept for a week. Her eyes closed slowly and then opened again and then she talked, slowly and firmly.

»Rico. Listen. I know you would really like a father. And I wish **for both of our sakes** that there was one here, believe me! But that doesn't mean I'm going to fall for every man you think might fit the job description.«

Oh well, so she thought Mr Lake was awful. Maybe it had something to do with her job in the nightclub. She was always being chatted up some bloke or other. Perhaps she just didn't want to do the same stuff at home. But if Mum wasn't careful, she might suddenly find herself having a grey day. Up until now she had never brought a boyfriend home,

---

windowsill – Fensterbank

for both of our sakes – um unser beider Willen

even though she met loads of men at work, a lot more than Mrs Dahling did behind the **meat counter**. One of them had to be right.

»OK. But what do you think of him? Please!« It was important to me that she liked Mr Lake, even if it was only a little bit. *I* liked him.

»Simon Westlake.« She thought hard. »Well, I … I'd say he's far and away the hottest thing I've met in my entire life.«

I wanted to be excited, for her and for me. But Mum just looked out of the window again. Now she not only looked tired but a little sad too, and even though she was right in front of me, she seemed far, far away like a lonely speck on the horizon. Sometimes I don't understand my mum at all.

> <u>HORIZON</u>: The spot right at the back of the world where earth and sky meet. Or is it the sea and the sky? It can't be the earth and the sea, that would have to be vertical, and then it would almost certainly be called something else. Like the searizon.

---

meat counter – Fleischtheke

MONDAY AGAIN

UP ON THE ROOF

I took Oskar out of our flat. The knot of men had untangled itself and there was nobody else to be seen. As I pulled the door shut behind me, I had a thought: »Who let you into the building, Oskar?«

His visor was up again. He took a deep breath, as though he had been expecting the question for ages and could now finally, finally give an answer. »Nobody. The front door was open!« he let out, **disgusted**. »Your neighbours should be more careful. Anybody could come in! Murderers, **burglars**, drunks who pee in the hallway. How can they be so *careless*!«

I shrugged. I had left the door to the building open a few times myself. It has a little hook at the back that clicks into a holder on the wall if you push it open hard. Not a big deal, unless your name is Oskar. In Oskar's life everything is dangerous – or at least he seems to think so.

»And how did you know which bell to ring?«

»From the list of names at the entrance.« His voice had gone all **squeaky** and rang up the stairs in front of us like a siren. »It was *open*!«

»Yes, all right, I heard you the first time.« I was becoming nervous. If he carried on like that, we'd bump into Mr Fitzke as well. I jumped up the stairs. »So, how did you work out my name?«

---

disgusted – angewidert

burglar – Einbrecher

squeaky – quietschend

He stumbled after me on his short legs, and finally he calmed down a little. »You said your father was Italian. Doretti is the only name on the list of names next to the doorbells that sounds Italian.«

I was annoyed that I hadn't thought of that myself, Oskar was very detectivey.

»Do you know Miss Marple?« I asked.

»No. Does she live here too?«

Ha! Now I could show him! Everybody knows the Miss Marple films! But maybe child prodigies don't watch television; they just appear on it, rattling off prime numbers on talent shows and stuff. I swallowed my not-very-nice-but-very-funny comment. If you like somebody, you shouldn't make fun of them, and Oskar could probably make fun of me ten times better than I could make fun of him, and he'd be able to find one hundred times more chances to do it. That made me think about little Sophia in Tempelhof with her moonface and the big, fat strawberry stain on her creased T-shirt – I bet she was really badly made fun of at her school.

»Don't run so fast!« Oskar wheezed. He was having difficulty keeping up. If his visor had been shut, it would have steamed up from all his breath. »Where are you taking me?«

Reluctantly I slowed down a little. We'd almost arrived at the fourth floor – Mr Fitzke's territory. And Mr Fitzke gets grumpy when it gets loud on the staircase. He hates noise even more than Mrs Dahling does.

»We're going up to the fifth floor,« I said in a low voice.

»What's up there?«

»The fifth floor, of course.«

»I mean, what are we going to do up there?«

I grinned. »You'll see. I hope you don't get dizzy.«

»*Dizzy?*« shrieked Oskar. He sounded like a wailing siren. »You're not taking me *up on the roof*?«

The next second, a door flew open and a wave of stinkiness **hit** us. Mr Fitzke was standing before us in his tattered striped pyjamas as if he'd just escaped from a **charity shop**. He hadn't shaved since I had last seen him on Saturday, or combed his hair, and he looked like a mop that had had an electric shock.

»Could you possibly be any louder?« he thundered. »I've got a heart complaint. What's all this noise about –« He stopped suddenly and stared in surprise at Oskar, who was at least three metres smaller than he was. Oskar quickly snapped his visor into place and stared back.

»What kind of strange creature are you? The dimwit has got himself a **sidekick** from the funny farm, has he?«

There was no reply.

»Can't you talk?« Mr Fitzke tapped on the helmet three times with his finger. »Hello? I asked you a question.«

»You stink!« Oskar suddenly shouted through the visor. »In developing countries lack of hygiene is one of the big-

---

to hit – hier: entgegenschlagen

charity shop – Second-Hand-Laden

sidekick – Kumpan

gest causes of illness! We have warm running water and soap. You should use it.«

Mr Fitzke eyed him as if he was an irritating insect he was about to squash with the palm of his hand. His gaze moved from Oskar's helmet to the bright red aeroplane on his shirt and back to the helmet. I held my breath.

»Who are you?« Mr Fitzke finally growled.

»Oskar. And you?«

»None of your business. And now buzz off before I rip your heads off and play football with them!«

That was the worst thing I had ever heard! Mr Fitzke spun around and the door went SLAM! Oskar took two quick steps forward, stretched out one hand and pressed the bell firmly.

»Don't do that!« I hissed. »He'll make mincemeat out of us if we annoy him again!« Either that or he really would rip our heads off.

»The bell's broken,« Oskar snorted, as if he hadn't heard me. He hammered on the door as though he wanted to break it down.

»What are you doing«?« I grabbed his wrist and pulled him away. I was beginning to get angry too.

»He's rude!« Oskar pushed up his visor. His face had gone as red as a tomato. »I'm not being treated like that just because I'm a child!«

»That's Mr Fitzke. It's just the way he is. He probably doesn't mean it.«

I was absolutely certain that Mr Fitzke did mean it, but

Oskar was angry enough already. »And I'm not a strange creature!« he roared through the closed door.

»He says that to everybody. You can't get upset about it,« I urged. »Now come on!«

In the end, he followed me. But as we were taking the last set of stairs up to the fifth floor, he kept turning around as though he expected Mr Fitzke **to pop up** again and chase after us. And he kept his right hand clenched in a fist until I had let us into the Runge-Blawetzkys' flat.

Before the RBs had zoomed off on holiday last Friday, they asked me if I'd water their houseplants and the flowers on the roof terrace for a little bit of pocket money. Of course, I said. I'd seen a new baseball cap I really wanted, although I probably won't buy it now after all. I've decided to put all my money in my piggy bank, just in case Mum has to buy the biggest possible piece of me from Mr 2000.

When you enter the RB's flat, you go through a large, open hallway into an even bigger living room and kitchen. There's a nice view from the windows over the **flat-roofed** St. Urban's Hospital and the surrounding streets, all the

to pop up – (plötzlich) auftauchen

flat roof – Flachdach

way over to Tempelhof. A narrow staircase leads directly up from the kitchen to the roof terrace. There's nothing else to see, though. They've closed off all the other rooms, even chubby Thorben's room, the one who always makes fun of me when nobody else is around. They probably think I'd go nosing around. They're so suspicious. Before they went away, they had put all of their houseplants on the kitchen table for watering. I steered Oskar past the table and up the stairs in front of me. He didn't even want to look around.

The roof terrace is the shape of a beach towel. When you go out of the terrace door, you can go over to the railing and look down into the backyard, or you can go to the other side and look down onto Dieffe. There are a few flowerpots and buckets with green stuff growing out of them. Most of the space is taken up by wooden chairs, a table and a bench, and if you have a **cushion** to put under your bum and a comic and a Coke, it's a nice place to sit. You can hear all the noises of the city, a never-ending, muffled humming, buzzing and hissing. And the view is phenomenal.

> PHENOMENAL: Brilliant, fantastic, unique, really cool. I knew this word already. But I'm writing it down here to show that I know some long words too.

---

cushion – Kissen

If you stand in the middle of the roof terrace, stretch out your arms and turn round in a circle, you can look out over Berlin in every direction. You can see hundreds of rooftops and the tops of thousands of green trees, the glass dome on the Reichstag, all kinds of church towers, the television tower on Alex, the **skyscrapers** on Potsdamer Platz and, a bit further on, the town hall in Schöneberg. In the sky above there's almost always an aeroplane that has taken off from Tempelhof or Tegel, or is landing. If you turn a little faster, all of these sights blur into one and you get dizzy. And if you turn *really* fast, you'll probably zoom over one of the railings along with a few of the flowerpots and race them to the bottom where you'll burst like a ripe tomato. Proper blood sauce and all the rest. Which is why I've never tried to go really fast. I'm not totally **bonkers**.

Oskar was not one bit impressed by any of it. He pressed his back to the terrace door and what you could see of his face through the helmet was very pale.

Even his voice was pale somehow. And **cross**.

»You said it would be great up here, not dangerous!«

»It is.«

I was giving up all hope of him taking off his helmet. What was the matter with him? I'd expected a person who only thought about squashed cyclists and run-over pedestrians to

---

skyscrapers – Wolkenkratzer

bonkers – bescheuert

cross – verärgert

be happy with a change of scene. And it wasn't dangerous up here, unless, of course, an aeroplane plopped down on the building. I thought about asking Oskar how much he knew about aeroplane crashes, but that probably wasn't a good idea.

»I've never been up on a roof,« he said in a whiney voice. »And now I know why.«

I pointed to the **railing** that looked out over Dieffe. »You haven't even been up to the edge. You can hold on to the railing.«

»I can swim,« he groaned, »but I still wouldn't jump into a pool full of piranhas.«

»What are piranhas?«

»Predatory fish with very sharp teeth from the *Serrasalmus* family. They live in the tropical freshwater of South America. They can rip an injured animal or a human to **shreds** in a few seconds.«

All right then. If I ever met one of the *Serra-wotsit* family, I would know where I stood. But …

»Are you terrified of everything?« I asked.

»I'm not terrified. I'm being cautious.«

I should have brought some Coke or lemonade. Maybe Oskar would have felt more comfortable up here then. I didn't want to run back down to the second floor, and the RBs' fridge, which I had peeked into by chance, was empty. Completely cleared out. How mean was that!

---

railing – Geländer

shred – Fetzen, Stückchen

»I'm just being cautious,« Oskar repeated quietly. »It's the instinct for **self-preservation**. You know – keeping yourself alive.«

I looked at him helplessly. I had brought him up here for a reason. I was starting to suspect he wouldn't be all that excited about my great idea, but seeing as we were up here already, I could at least try.

I pointed to the fold-up screen made of thick, tightly woven bamboo canes that separated the RB's roof terrace from the terrace next door.

»Would you like to look through the petition?«

»It's called a **partition**.«

»I know. I was just testing.«

Thank goodness he didn't look at me; otherwise he would have noticed right away that I'd gone bright red. Just then I would have liked to borrow his helmet.

> PARTITION: *Easily confused with a letter of complaint signed by lots of people, which is also a difficult word to learn. A partition is like a wall that protects you from draughts and nosy neighbours.*

---

self-preservation – Selbsterhaltung

partition – Trennwand

»What's behind there?« said Oskar.

»Mr Marrak's roof terrace.«

»Who?«

»One of the three men you bumped into on the staircase. The one in the red uniform with the golden safe on it. He has his own business.« I took a deep breath without him noticing. »Alarms, Safes and Locks: Sales, Service and Installation.«

I said the sentence calmly as if I was picking a **daisy** from a **meadow**, but really I had almost fainted with the effort. Now I was bursting with pride because I hadn't made a single mistake. Mr Marrak had once given me one of his business cards. I had studied it at least ten times a day every day for a week and learned it all off by heart so that I could impress somebody one day. I never dreamed that it would be **cleverclogs** Oskar.

But all Oskar said was, »I see«.

Honestly! He can really ruin a good mood. On the other hand I should have known that long complicated things are easy-peasy for a child prodigy. How do they manage to know so much and remember new things straight away? And is there anything they don't know?

»How far away from the earth is the moon?« I asked.

»Just under four hundred thousand kilometres.«

---

daisy – Gänseblümchen

meadow – Wiese

cleverclogs – Klugscheißer

Aha! His answer came as quick as a shot, but just under is not quite the same as all the way there, and before you know it, you could end up landing on Mars, Jupiter or Uranus, instead of on the moon.

> <u>URANUS</u>: On photos it's as blue as Oskar's crash helmet. At first I wrote YOURANUS, but it seems that the automatic correction thing works after all.

»The exact average distance,« said Oskar next to me, slowly, »is three hundred and eighty-four thousand, four hundred and one kilometres.«

OK, **one nil to** Oskar. But I didn't want to give up completely. »But you had to think about, didn't you?«

»I thought you wanted to know how far the moon is from the earth today. But to know that we would first have to ascertain the daily parallax; and you can only do that if –«

»Don't worry about it.« I gave up. »So, do you want to look at the other roof terrace or not?«

»Why?«

»Because I want to show you something. It's not one bit dangerous!« I added quickly, before he could start the siren thing again. »We just have to be a bit careful because Mr

---

one nil to – eins zu null für

Marrak has only just come home. He might want to lie on his terrace in this nice weather.«

Finally, Oskar let go of the door and came to join me by the partition. He shoved right up next to me and helped me push the **bamboo** canes apart so we could see through to the other side. Mr Marrak's roof terrace is a lot larger than the RBs'. There are more plants, fancier furniture, and the floor is made of thick, beautifully streaked wooden planks, much nicer than the RBs' red-brown **tiles**.

»Cool,« whispered Oskar. His fingers were short and his nails were tiny and bitten. Not even the smallest of Mum's nail stickers would have fitted onto them.

»What's that over there, that house-shaped thing with the pointed roof?« he said. »The one right at the back on the left?«

»Which one is left again?«

I almost bit my tongue. I didn't mean to ask that. It just slipped out. I could see the stupid little house right in front of me, or its roof at least, because the entrance was hidden on both sides by more bamboo.

But Oskar simply said: »Left is where you see the little roof.«

»Of course. I knew that. It's the top of the staircase of the next building – the one behind this one. Mr Marrak let me peek in once when I was in his flat. You used to be able to

---

bamboo – Bambus

tiles – Kacheln

get into it from here, but you can't anymore. The door to the little house is locked because there was a gas explosion. Since then the building's been **condensed**.«

Oskar turned his head towards me with a jerk. He almost sliced off my ear with his open visor. »It's been what?«

»Condensed. If you hear so badly under your funny helmet –«

»It's **condemned**, not condensed.«

»That's what I said.«

»You didn't.«

»I did.«

»You did!«

»I didn't!«

Oskar wrinkled his nose triumphantly. »You see.«

Something had gone wrong in all the fast words, but I didn't have time to think about what it was.

»Oh, never mind!« I pointed to the little house with the locked door. »Anyway, that's where we're going, in there.«

»Into the building that's been condemned?«

I nodded.

»Now you've really gone crazy. If it's condemned, that means it could be about to fall down.«

Flippin' heck! All I wanted was to see for myself that there were no shadowier shadows. And no Miss Bonhöfer. With

---

to condense – verdichten, zusammenpressen

to condemn – etw. für abbruchreif erklären

Oskar by my side it wouldn't be scary, it would just be the two of us on a big adventure.

»And the building is just as locked up as that little house over there,« Oskar gestured at the pointy roof, »so there's absolutely no chance. What do you think I am: a burglar?«

»I thought we could ask Mr Marrak for a key. He could come with us. We could see if there's anything still lying around in the empty flats.« That was my last, useless attempt. »A few cool old things. That kind of stuff.«

»Forget it.«

He wouldn't change his mind and that made me cross. »Are you scared again?« I said, facing up to him.

»It's got nothing to do with being scared. It's about being sensible.«

»Ah, you see!«

»You're a real pain in the neck, do you know that?« said Oskar with a sigh. He took a deep breath and went over to the railing from which you can look down into the backyard. Carefully, he leaned over it, but only a little bit. He even stood on his **tiptoes** and began to rock gently, as though he was listening to music no one else could hear.

When I saw him standing there, something strange happened. I thought of Molly One and Molly Two. Molly One was my fifth birthday present from Mum. I'd never seen a hamster before, or I might have seen one but forgotten. In any case I thought Molly was great. She waddled around

---

tiptoes – Zehenspitzen

and sniffed the air with her tiny pink nose. Mum had put her in a small straw basket and tied a yellow **ribbon** around her middle.

»There's a cage, of course. I've hidden it in the living room. Hang on one second, love.«

I nodded happily and took Molly out of the basket. I'd never held something as small and warm and alive as that before. I pressed her to my chest because I loved her so much, and there was a **crack**.

I got Molly Two a week later because I couldn't stop crying. She moved into the cage meant for Molly One. Mum and I buried Molly One in a small park. I can't remember its name. I hope she's OK there.

Molly Two was around for a lot longer than Molly One. Mum kept on reminding me that I shouldn't hold her too tightly, so I didn't squeeze this time. But I let her run around in my room until one day she disappeared and was never seen again.

»That's it,« Mum said, after we'd turned the whole flat upside down at least three times. »No more hamsters. I think, Frederico, you're not yet ready to take responsibility for a small creature. Sorry. It was my mistake.«

Oskar had finished rocking and turned towards me.

»There you go. Happy now?«

»Not bad for starters,« I said generously.

---

ribbon – Band

there was a crack – es machte knack

»What about you?« He looked at me. »Aren't you afraid of anything?«

»Yes. I'm afraid I could get lost in the city,« I admitted. »I can't find my way, you know. With all those lefts and rights and stuff.«

»Has that ever happened?«

»Nah, I've never been very far by myself. It wouldn't actually be that bad. Mum says if I ever get lost, I should get in a taxi and let them bring me home. If she's not in, somebody in the building will lend me the money.«

»Good idea. And apart from getting lost?«

I shook my head. I had to be careful. There was something I was more afraid of than getting lost, and I had already been thinking that I would have to tell Oskar as soon as we became **proper** friends. But I wasn't sure if he really was my proper friend already. I would have to check.

»Are you coming back tomorrow?« I asked him.

I felt my head go red with excitement. That was quite a clever test, I thought. Proper friends always have time for one another. They want to have as many adventures together as possible. If Oskar said no …

He looked at me carefully, like I was something on a shelf in the supermarket that he wasn't sure he wanted to buy. He scratched his arm. He **fingered** his aeroplane badge. He chewed on his lower lip with those large teeth of his.

---

proper – richtig

to finger – befummeln

»Actually,« he said, »I've got plans for tomorrow. They could take all day.«

My heart almost hit the tiled floor on the RBs' terrace. But only almost. At the last second Oskar changed his mind. »But I can probably do that another time,« he said quickly.

I stretched one arm out in relief. »Are we proper friends now?«

He placed his little hand into mine. It was really warm. He smiled. »Isn't that what we've been the whole time?«

I'm sitting here writing. Normally I would have been asleep for a long time by now, but Mum has gone out with Irina and her new toenails – she did put new stickers on after all, small, white daisies with really tiny yellow pollen thingies in the middle (I'm not going to look up the word now). And she said I could go to bed whenever I felt like it. It is the holidays after all. Now I'm sitting here and I have to write down everything that I'm thinking about so that I remember it tomorrow.

First of all I have to say that today was at least half a success. Oskar's my friend now, even if he **has a screw loose**, and Mum thinks that Mr Lake is the hottest thing she's ever

---

to have a screw loose – eine Schraube locker haben

seen, even though she doesn't want to flirt with him. Flirting is when you go out with somebody; then you fall in love, get married and make babies. I could tell Mum that I'm not bothered about the order and then she might see things differently and invite Mr Lake to bingo tomorrow after all.

Hopefully!

Earlier, I sat in the thinking chair and looked out of the window. The moon is still quite full and if you turn your head a bit, you can see it between the branches of those trees with the funny peeling bark. Today the moon is completely orange. It's probably on fire up there just under four hundred thousand kilometres away. So I was sitting there, thinking about the day, and I suddenly asked myself what was going on today in the stairway when everybody crashed into each other. I mean, today was Monday! It's normal for Mr Marrak to be around at that time of day – he can do what he wants with his time because he has his own business – but what was somebody like Mr Lake doing at home? He must have some kind of a job; otherwise he couldn't rent such an expensive flat. Was he on holiday or what? And Mr Kiesling too – out and about in the middle of the day when he should have been making teeth in Tempelhof.

Very strange.

I'm really looking forward to tomorrow! Oskar is coming and we're going to go for a walk by the canal, even if Oskar doesn't know it yet. It'll be great. If the weather's nice, maybe we'll have an ice cream. Nah, we'll have an ice cream whatever the weather. And then I'll tell Oskar what my greatest fear is and where it comes from. I'll tell him the story of how my dad died.

TUESDAY

UP AND DOWN

Sometimes you wake up in the morning, open your eyes and think of something beautiful right away. It's as though a small sun is rising inside you, making you all warm and bright.

Oskar and I had arranged to meet at ten o'clock. I **snuggled** up in bed and pictured us walking along the canal together. When I'm alone, I only ever go straight over the Admiralsbrücke to school because as soon as I lose sight of things I know, it's over and out. I'd get lost in a supermarket if it only had one **aisle**. I'm a hopeless case.

But today Oskar would be with me. We could turn left and right wherever we liked. We could walk far, far down the canal, somewhere I'd never been before. With a child prodigy at your side, far, far away is a piece of cake. Even if you do get lost, your friend can ask somebody the way and he'll remember what people tell him, left and right and all the rest of it. It would be a piece of cake with icing on top!

I saw the wall of the building behind shimmering through the window. There were no shadows from the clouds. It would be a lovely day with Oskar. And this evening I was going to bingo with Mum. Maybe I could persuade her to take Mr Lake along after all. Or I could ask Mr Lake if he felt like turning up without an invitation. He could pretend he was looking for his helpless old mother, who'd got lost

---

to snuggle – kuscheln

aisle – Gang

while shopping in a supermarket with only one aisle. What if he never found her, the poor woman? What a mystery!

I looked at my Mickey Mouse alarm clock. Almost nine o'clock – I still had an hour. Then again it could also be quarter to twelve, because sometimes I confuse Mickey's short and long arms, but I never wake up that late, not even in the holidays and I was sure Oskar would have rung the bell if I had overslept.

I jumped out of bed, went to the loo and tiptoed past Mum's bedroom into the kitchen to get a bowl of **granola** and a glass of orange juice. Ten minutes later I'd had my breakfast, cleaned my teeth and was dressed and ready to go.

Much too early.

If I'm waiting for something or I don't really know what to do with myself, I sit in the thinking chair in the living room. I can't remember when Mum and I **christened** it the thinking chair but we really love it. It's big and cosy. Sometimes I need it to calm down the lottery barrel. But it's also great to sit in and read comics and to look out of the window at the leaves of the trees moving in the wind. Sometimes sparrows sit in the trees' branches, chirping at each other excitedly. You can think up stories with heroes like O and his wooden horse, or you can think about important questions such as whether Miss Marple will ever

---

granola – Knuspermüsli

to christen – taufen

marry Mr Stringer. He's her best friend. He's **clumsy** and too stupid for Miss Marple, but she's got nobody else to fall in love with, apart from the fat stable owner, who puts his hand on her knee any chance he gets.

Hours later, when Mum got out of bed, I was still sitting in the thinking chair. I'd already jumped up a hundred times, run to the window and looked out over Dieffe. At one point I saw Mr Marrak leaving the house and walking off, on the way to his car, which was parked somewhere nearby. But that was it.

No crash helmet anywhere.

No little spot of blue.

No Oskar.

I dragged myself over to Mum in the kitchen, in such a bad mood that I felt as heavy and sad as an elephant. Elephants go into the jungle to die. They go to a place where other elephants have died before them; and before those elephants, other elephants who were looking for a place to die near other dead elephants. A giant elephant **graveyard**.

Our kitchen was not a graveyard, but I had to go somewhere. I sat at the table and moaned about my bad luck. Mum poured herself a coffee and sat across from me.

»He **stood you up**, eh?«

---

clumsy – ungeschickt

graveyard – Friedhof

to stand sb. up – jmd. sitzenlassen, jmd. versetzen

I wasn't sure what she meant. Oskar had been standing up when he left the building yesterday, but I couldn't remember if I was standing up or sitting down? That couldn't be what she meant. But instead of saying something, I nodded quickly. Sometimes I'm embarrassed to show Mum that I don't get things.

»Well, it looks as though both of us are having a bad start to the day,« she continued. »I have to go away for two or three days.«

And that was that. There were dark shadows under her eyes. Maybe she'd slept badly. I looked at her, waiting. She looked back. She sipped her coffee. Finally she sighed.

»Do you understand, love? I've got to leave this afternoon. That means there won't be any bingo for us this evening.«

That means … *what?!*

»I'm sorry, Rico! I know how much you were looking forward to it.«

Great, no bingo either! She probably wanted to do a tour of all the hairdressers in the city with her friend Irina to get new hints put in her hair. Well, I was used to being left standing up and all alone. One day Mum would come home after a **pipe** had burst or something and I would be lying drowned in the hall, next to a letter telling her that I had to repeat the school year. It would serve her right!

»Where are you going?« I asked her grumpily.

»Do you remember Uncle Christian?«

---

pipe – Rohr

Only a little bit. I don't like him at all. Uncle Christian is Mum's older brother, he lives somewhere in Germany down at the bottom and left. A few years ago, before we moved into this flat, when we still lived in Neukölln, he visited us. He and Mum had such a fight that I hid under my bed. He left that same day. I couldn't remember what he looked like any more or how his voice sounded.

»Yes, he's not very nice,« I said. »What's about him?«

»He's not very well. I have to go and see him.«

»Why? What's the matter?«

»Cancer.«

Everybody knows what cancer is, even Forrest Gump. If Mum was saying such a serious word as though there was nothing to it, then something was wrong. She said cancer as **cheerfully** as Mrs Dahling would say *A tiny bit more perhaps?* at the meat counter.

»Will he die?« I asked slowly.

»Yes. He might.«

If the train takes a long time, Uncle Christian might be dead when she arrives, then our bingo game will have been cancelled for nothing.

»Do you have to go today?« I said.

»Oh, for God's sake!« Mum shouted at me just like that. »Do you have to be so self-centred? Can't you think about somebody else for a change?«

---

cheerfully – fröhlich

SELF-CENTREDNESS: When you only think about yourself. There's also the opposite thing, when you only think about other people, and if you can do that you're a saint. But saints usually get treated badly and burned at the stake. It's important to find a middle way so that you get what you want and make other people happy at the same time.

Mum poured herself another coffee without looking at me. She took a sip. She started to cry. It was as though a rain cloud had squeezed its way into the kitchen. I can't bear it when Mum cries. The world looks as dark as if God has switched off the light.

I should probably have noticed much earlier that something wasn't right, because even her Japanese **dressing gown** hung off her sadly. Instead of thinking about Mum, I had been busy with my own problems. When I saw her crying, I was sorry I'd thought up the burst pipe story. Somebody not turning up and a cancelled bingo evening are not as bad as a dying brother, even if you can't stand him. Mum's unhappiness was bigger than mine.

I got up, went around the table and put my arms around her. Mum buried her face in my shoulder. Her hair smelled of a mixture of shampoo and the nightclub. She held me so

dressing gown – Bademantel

tight I could barely breathe. That's how Molly One must have felt right before the crack.

Just when I thought I couldn't take it any longer, she let go of me. She drew the back of her hand across her eyes. »I'll make it up to you, love, I promise,« she sniffed. »But right now –«

»It's OK.«

»You'll have to take care of yourself for a few days. You'll manage, won't you? You're a big boy.«

»Of course.«

»I'll leave you some money, and if you need anything, you go and see Mrs Dahling, all right? I'll try and call her at Karstadt, maybe they can bring her to the phone.«

»Don't worry. I'll go and see her this evening and tell her myself.«

»OK. Remember you can call me any time on my mobile.« She took hold of me by the shoulders, pushed me a little distance away from her and looked into my eyes. »I love you more than anything! You know that, don't you?«

I really wanted to say I was sorry and tell her I hadn't meant to say what I said, but suddenly I was all mixed up. I'd just thought of something terrible and not even the lottery balls in my head were working properly. They clacked together for a moment or two then lay still as though they were frozen. The terrible thought was this: if Mum's brother had cancer, maybe she'd get it too, because she –

»Rico?«

»Hm?« Tears were running down my cheeks and snot was **dribbling** out of my nose and I didn't have a tissue.

»Cancer isn't catching. Do you hear me?«

I snorted something.

»You don't have to worry about that.«

I snorted again, but I felt better. Mum never lies to me. She raised one hand and wiped my face with the sleeve of her dressing gown. She finally had a smile on her face, even if it was as faint as a **snail's tracks**.

»Christian phoned very early this morning,« she explained. »Then I couldn't fall asleep but I must have dozed off and now it's late and the train leaves at two-thirty. I wish I could do something about your little friend with the helmet, but I still have to pack, have a shower, sort myself out and buy a ticket at the station …«

»Go on,« I said.

I watched her as she stumbled out of the kitchen past her bedroom. The door was open. I could see her **four-poster bed** with the fancy, shiny sheets and the posters of dolphins and whales on the walls.

I slowly calmed down. Mum wasn't getting cancer, we'd go to bingo next Tuesday and Oskar would turn up at some point. I remembered that he'd said he had something important to do today. Maybe that was more important than

---

to dribble – tröpfeln

snail's track – Schneckenspur

four-poster bed – Himmelbett

taking a walk by the canal and he would turn up later. And even if he came tomorrow or the day after tomorrow, I still had something to look forward to: Mrs Dahling would definitely feed me canapés this evening and we'd watch television together, even though it wasn't a weekend! If I could persuade her to watch a Miss Marple film, that was almost as good as playing bingo. I wouldn't be able to persuade her to play bingo though. Mrs Dahling thinks bingo is for old **fogies** who hitch their trousers up under their **armpits**.

Life had just been shadowier than the shadowiest shadowy shadows. Now it was bright again. I felt bad for a minute that I didn't feel sorry for Uncle Christian, but he shouldn't have shouted the way he did when he'd argued with Mum. I had been so afraid that I had hidden under the bed and that's where I'd found Molly Two. She was right at the back in an old trainer I'd grown out of. Maybe she'd been looking for other hamsters back there.

The trainer stank.

Shortly after two o'clock Mum's taxi arrived. I went downstairs with her. The driver stashed her large suitcase in the

---

fogies – komische Käuze

armpits – Achseln

boot. Mum blew me a kiss from the back seat and then they drove off. I waved after her. I almost thought I could see the sad, black rain cloud floating after the taxi.

I went upstairs and sat back down in the thinking chair for a while. I didn't know what I was going to do until the evening. I could water the RBs' flowers, but what if Oskar turned up just when I was upstairs on the fifth floor?

But Oskar wasn't going to turn up.

It was my own fault. I should have asked him for his telephone number or at least what his surname was so that I could look it up in the phone book. I didn't really know anything about him, not even where he lived.

»It's your own fault,« I repeated, quietly.

Now I would have to spend the entire day by myself until I went to Mrs Dahling's in the evening.

I read a comic.

I drank orange juice.

I ran downstairs to the first floor and rang Berts' bell.

Berts is great fun, but he wasn't at home. Just my luck. And if Oskar had turned up in the meantime and rung the bell, double bad luck, but then I could at least drop in on old Mr Mommsen, the caretaker, on the ground floor. He tells exciting stories sometimes, like the one where Miss Bonhöfer exploded, and he always has some chocolate in the cupboard. But mostly he's just drunk and it's the booze talking.

---

boot – Kofferraum

BOOZE: Everything that makes you drunk. Alcohol. Usually the cheaper stuff. After drinking it most people spout nonsense, which is what is meant by »it's the booze talking«. I didn't have to look that up. Some things you can work out all by yourself.

Mr Mommsen is a **widower** and fat and he doesn't have nice teeth. He probably doesn't clean them properly. Jule once said he was an old goat and no woman would be interested in him, so he probably has grey days too. If today was one of his grey days and if it spread to Mrs Dahling's flat, I wasn't sure I could cope. After Mum's rain cloud and my own elephant feeling, I'd had enough sadness for one day.

So I went back upstairs.

There was nothing happening on the stairs. It was so quiet in the building that it was almost a bit **creepy**. Normally there's noise coming from somewhere: Berts and Jule and Massoud have their music turned up, or the Kessler twins are screaming at each other, or there's some classical tra-la-la from Mr Kiesling's flat. You can even hear noise coming from the very top floor when the RBs' chubby son Thorben brings his friends home and plays PlayStation with

---

widower – Witwer

creepy – unheimlich

them with the volume turned up. Mr Fitzke has complained a hundred times but it doesn't stop them.

Today there was **zilch**. Absolute quiet.

I went back into the flat.

I turned the TV on and five minutes later I turned it off.

I put my dirty washing in the washing machine.

I made my bed.

I sat on my bed.

Boring.

There was no point waiting. Oskar wasn't coming. And if he did come, he could jump in the canal. I wasn't going to let the RBs' flowers die of thirst just because of him.

So up I went.

By the time I got to the top, I wasn't angry at Oskar anymore. It wasn't his fault that I was bored. It wasn't his fault that our walk along the canal filled up my head like a balloon and that there wasn't any room for anything else.

Most of the RBs' plants were still wet enough. I watered the rest.

Then I went back downstairs.

I bumped into Mr Marrak between the third and second floors. He was wearing his fancy red work clothes and carrying his washing bag, which was full to **bursting**. The first time Mrs Dahling saw him struggling with it, she put both hands to her head. »Typical man!« she'd said. »He waits until

---

zilch – nichts (ugs.)

to burst – platzen

he's down to his last pair of underpants and his last shirt and then his girlfriend's supposed to stay up all night just so he has something to wear!« Nobody has ever seen his girlfriend at Dieffe 93, but clearly Mr Marrak doesn't have a washing machine.

»Hello, Mr Marrak«, I said and tried to get past him.

»Hi Rico.« He put his washing bag down with some effort and nodded at me. »Are you wandering around again? Whose flat are you **nosying** at today?«

He didn't mean it **nastily**. When I went to look at his flat after we had moved in, he even offered me a Coke. Of course by then Mum had already told him that I was a child proddity and that the reason I liked to look at other people's flats was because I could only keep going straight on the street and didn't get to see much of the world. Mum had told everybody in the building, and apart from Mr Fitzke all the neighbours were very kind and let me in when I knocked on their door. Some of them let me in a few times, like Mrs Dahling or Berts, Jule and Massoud. The Kesslers have asked a couple of times if I want to pop in again, but their twins get on my nerves.

Last time I went to Mr Marrak's he even gave me his business card, the one with the golden safe on it. Now when we bump into each other, we're very polite, but he's never invited me into his flat again. I always hope that one day

---

nosy – neugierig

nastily – garstig

he'll open the little white house on the roof terrace with one of his many keys, but it doesn't seem likely. Grown-ups are always worrying about doing things that are illegal.

> <u>ILLEGAL</u>: When you're not allowed to do something because it's forbidden and the police might not like it. LEGAL means it's allowed (and OOPS means that you've done something you're not allowed to and are hoping nobody will notice).

»I was watering the Runge-Blawetzkys' flowers,« I explained to Mr Marrak. »They're on holiday.«

»Who?«

»What?«

»The flowers or the Runge-Blawetzkys?«

I looked at him, **puzzled**. Was he winding me up? Since when do houseplants go on holiday?

He was grinning. »Just teasing. A Rico tease. Don't you get it?«

He must have a screw loose!

»Didn't even notice that my lovely neighbours had **taken off**,« he added as though nothing had happened.

---

puzzled – verdutzt

to take off – abheben, hier: abzischen, wegfahren

I would have liked to tell him he wasn't likely to notice when he spent all day running here, there and everywhere with his jangling bunch of keys, carrying his stinky underwear around in a huge laundry bag. What an idiot!

»Don't look so cross!« He thumped my arm. »It was just a joke. A bit of fun from one man to another. I didn't mean to upset you. Sorry, OK?«

»OK,« I said slowly.

I don't like having my leg pulled. But in this case I would make an exception and I decided to be only a little bit cross because Mr Marrak is usually friendly to me. But that was as far as I would go. He's big and tall and has a chunky face, but otherwise there's nothing unusual about him. He isn't a good choice for Mum. He already has a girlfriend after all and it wouldn't be much fun for Mum, washing his clothes while he went out with another woman. And then there'd be cleaning and tidying up and everything. Mr Marrak is very messy. When I visited his flat it looked like a bomb had hit it. If he wasn't careful, he'd let himself go and end up like Mr Fitzke in front of the cheese counter at the supermarket.

»Right, let's get back to it, shall we?« He bent down to pick up the bag of washing. »Say hello to your mum from me.«

»I can't, she's gone away for a few days.«

He stopped what he was doing, stood up straight again and looked at me. »And who's keeping an eye on you till she gets back?«

»Me and Mrs Dahling.«

»I see.« His bottom lip was sticking out as if he didn't like what he'd heard. »To be perfectly truthful, I don't understand some parents. They bring children into the world and then **leave them to their own devices** all day, either in front of the telly or the computer –«

»I don't spend all day sitting in front of –«

»Or they let their little ones **romp** around alone. If you ask me, Mr 2000 should be a lesson to them all!«

»My mother doesn't leave me –«

»If those children who were kidnapped hadn't been running around alone in the big city, nobody would have been able to snatch them! That's just my opinion, of course!«

Now I was cross again, but instead of answering back, I just nodded. I should have stuck up for Mum, but Mr Marrak wasn't listening to me anyway. His pale face had gone all pink and looked like one of Mum's bath sponges. If I said anything, he would just carry on complaining and when he'd finally had enough, he might ask me to help him carry his bag.

»I've got to go,« I said.

»Me too,« he said, finally balancing the bag of washing on his shoulder. »Take care.«

»Yup.«

I jumped down the final steps to the second floor. As I let myself into the flat, I could hear Mr Marrak huffing and

---

to leave sb. to their own devices – jmd. sich selbst überlassen

romp – herumtollen

puffing his way up the stairs. »Bloody fifth floor,« he grumbled. »Next time I'm moving in somewhere with a lift!«

It's his own fault, I thought. He should buy himself a washing machine!

I'd only been back in the flat a few seconds when the **boredom** picked up where it had left off.

I sat in the thinking chair.

I flicked through the dictionary and learned three new words.

I looked out of the window and snoozed.

I forgot the three new words.

I went into the kitchen and drank some more juice.

I ate some more granola.

I washed up the glass and the cereal bowl and the spoon.

My eyes fell on the bin. The bag was full to the brim – something to do! If I took the rubbish out to the yard and then wrote in my diary, the afternoon would go much faster.

So I went back downstairs again.

The giant bins are in the backyard, along the wall we share with the building next door. You have to pull quite hard on one half of the large double door that leads into the backyard, because it's been sticking for a few weeks. The other half doesn't open at all. Mr Mommsen, the caretaker, should have **mended** it long ago because it's just getting

---

boredom – Langeweile

to mend – reparieren

worse. but he's too busy boozing. Even the bin men have complained about it.

I tugged at the sticking door until I could just about fit through with my bag of rubbish and I crashed straight into Mr Mommsen. He was armed with a large brush and a small dustpan. I remembered that Tuesday was his day to sweep the yard, whether he was drunk or not.

»Hello, Mr Mommsen,« I said.

He staggered a little and stared at me. »Who are you?«

»Rico Doretti. Second floor.«

»I know that,« he said. »Do you think I'm stupid or what?«

Can you believe it?

Instead of answering him, I held the door open for him as wide as I could manage. He pushed past me and looked me right in the face. His eyes were **milky**.

»The door could do with fixing,« I said.

»Go and play!« he snapped.

»I will. See you later!«

»I hope not.«

The door clicked shut in slow motion. I shook my head briefly and went over to the bin. I pushed up the heavy black lid and threw in the bag of rubbish and then I saw it. In the middle of the dirty, pongy mess lay a small, bright red aeroplane.

I looked up at the sky, as I had done when I had found the piece of pasta. Dark clouds were forming and pushing

---

milky – milchig (hier: trübe)

themselves in front of the sun. Right up at the top, on the RBs' roof terrace, a final ray of sun glinted on the metal railing. I looked down again. There was only one way that the little aeroplane could have landed down here: it must have come loose from Oskar's shirt when he was standing up there yesterday, showing me he wasn't afraid. The aeroplane must have spun down into the yard and somebody must have picked it up and thrown it away. It had probably been drunken Mr Mommsen, just a few minutes ago.

I stood on my tiptoes and tried to fish the aeroplane out of the bin without getting dirty. It took a while, but finally I **reached** it. There was no dirt on it. I tapped the broken-off wing; then I put it into my trouser pocket and grinned. Oskar would be really happy when I gave him back his badge! He was probably missing it already.

Then I went back up to the second floor where my diary was waiting for me. Now I'm looking forward to a nice evening with Mrs Dahling and canapés! Which means I have to go back *up* and then back *down* again.

Flippin' heck!

---

to reach – erreichen

Flippin' heck! – Verdammter Mist!

ALMOST WEDNESDAY

THE SPECIAL EDITION

About ten minutes ago both of Mickey Mouse's arms showed twelve. So it's already after midnight.

In the building behind ours an enormous shadowier shadow has just moved, I'm sure of it. That's why I've moved from my room into the living room, into the thinking chair.

All the lights are on, but even if they were off, you still couldn't see the moon through the window. It's darkest night outside. A stormy wind is moving the branches of the trees, rustling their leaves and driving a drizzly rain against the **windowpanes**.

I've brought my **duvet** with me and have covered my legs with it. I'm sitting in front of the computer writing my diary. I have to write down what happened this evening right away, otherwise I won't be able to get to sleep. And I have to think up a plan.

If only I could think more quickly.

Mrs Dahling knows nothing.

If I call Mum, I'll just worry her.

It's up to me.

I'm really scared.

windowpanes – Fensterscheiben

duvet – Bettdecke

Shortly before seven thirty I went upstairs to Mrs Dahling. I didn't want to miss the local evening news. Well, actually I didn't want to miss the canapés but saying I didn't want to miss the evening news sounds less greedy.

Anyway, I rang Mrs Dahling's bell. No reply. I pressed my ear to the door and listened. Nothing. Then I remembered. Mrs Dahling and I almost always see each other on Saturdays, which is her day off. But I'd completely forgotten that during the week she works until eight. She couldn't be home yet. At that very moment she was probably standing behind the meat counter butchering the final **pork chop**. Sometimes I can be such an idiot!

On the floor above me somebody was crunching around on the stairs. Then I heard a cheerful little whistle. It couldn't be Mr Fitzke; he has to be the least **cheerful** person on the planet. A door fell shut. Then there was silence.

So I went up to the fourth floor. A heavy blue bag of rubbish was sitting in the stairway. Strips of wallpaper and cling film splattered with red and yellow and orange were **peeking out**. Great! Mr Lake was at home, and I had half an hour to spare. If I went about it the right way, I was sure he would let me into his flat.

When I rang, he opened the door immediately. There he was with his amazing white teeth and his black hair and the

---

pork chop – Schweinekotelett

cheerful – fröhlich

to peek out – hervorschauen

scar on his chin. He looked at me in **astonishment**. With concern, almost.

»Rico! Has something happened?«

Why do so many people ask if something has happened when a child rings their doorbell?

I shook my head and stretched out a hand. »Good evening! My name is Frederico Doretti. I'm –«

»Ehm … I know who you are.«

He wouldn't let me finish! Some people can't even keep quiet for ten seconds, and what I had to say was almost as difficult as the thing about Mr Marrak's Alarms, Safes and Locks business. Somewhere in my head a small **switch** flicked on almost by itself and started up the lottery machine. I was hot and uncomfortable. I dropped my hand. I'd have to forget about shaking his. You can't concentrate on everything at the same time after all, and up until now Mum had always said this bit for me.

»My name is Frederico Doretti!« I repeated in a loud voice. »I'm a child proddity! That's why I can only walk straight ahead and don't see much of the world!« I got faster and faster. »That's why I like looking at other people's flats *canicomeinplease*?«

Suddenly I wanted to turn on my heels and run away. If you knew ten seconds before you said or did something how stupid you would feel ten seconds later, you probably

---

astonishment – Erstaunen

switch – Schalter

wouldn't say or do quite a lot of what you do say and do. But it was too late now.

»Child proddity?« Mr Lake's eyebrows had slid together in the middle.

»That means, I can think a lot, but not particularly quickly,« I squeezed out a further sentence.

»Ohhh-kay,« he said, very slowly.

»But that doesn't mean I'm stupid. For example, the moon is three hundred and eighty-four thousand, four hundred and one kilometres away from the earth. On average.«

»I see.« Very slowly again.

»The day before yesterday I didn't know that and it's quite likely I'll forget it again soon. Sometimes a few things go missing from my brain, but I don't know when and where until it happens.«

»Well, if that's the way things are ...« Mr Lake was smiling now, and it was a nice smile. He pulled the door open towards him. »Come on in.«

About time!

I pushed past him and he closed the door. The smell of paint hit my nose. There were boxes right down the corridor, most of them piled up on top of other boxes, some of them closed, others open.

»I hope you don't mind a bit of mess,« Mr Lake said. »I'm still moving in.«

I shook my head. The mess was perfectly OK, as long as he could get used to things being tidy, just in case he married Mum.

The door next to me stood open, so I went in. It was the living room, and it looked like winter itself in there. Instead of a carpet there was a wooden floor, painted white. The walls were white and so were the shelves. The shelves were only half full, with books and CDs standing and lying on them. I couldn't see a picture or a poster anywhere; there were no nice **ornaments** like there were in Mrs Dahling's or ours. There was a white leather sofa with a table in front of it. An empty glass was standing on an open BILD newspaper. The bottom of the glass was wet and had made a wavy **stain** right across a picture of somebody called Cindy. Cindy comes from Hohenschönhausen, it said in big letters, is twenty-two and a **nail technician**. You could see her boobs. Apart from that there were all kinds of things scattered across the table: pens, a notebook, till receipts and so on. In one corner of the room a small TV was standing on the floor, in the other corner a stereo system.

»**Everything fine and dandy**?« Mr Lake said behind me.

It sounded like the kind of question you ask when you don't know what else to say. It also sounded like a question you can only answer with a yes, so I murmured yes.

---

ornament – Verzierung

stain – Fleck

nail technician – hier: Fußpflegerin

everything fine and dandy – alles schön und gut

DANDY: Somebody like Mr Kiesling from the third floor who's got a lot of clothes and spends a lot of time in front of the mirror. I washed my face and put on a clean T-shirt before leaving the flat, so maybe that's what Mr Lake meant.

I folded my hands behind my back and looked up at the ceiling. At least the ceiling was pretty, very pretty in fact – old-fashioned **plaster stucco**, and the only part of the room that was painted in a colour.

»How's your mum?«

The ceiling looked a bit like a rainforest. There were all kinds of flowers and leaves in orange and yellow and red wrapped up in each other. A few of them looked so real they could have been growing down from the ceiling. Mum would like it …

»Rico?«

»Hm?«

»Your mum.«

»She thinks you're the hottest thing she's ever met in her life. But …«

A bit of green in between the other colours would have been nice. Or something completely different from all the flowery, leafy things. I wonder if you could get stucco shapes

plaster stucco – Gipsstuck

with fish. Then your ceiling would look like an aquarium. You could have a turtle coming out of one corner and a bright little fish out of the other. And in the middle a blue whale, as big as –

Mr Lake cleared his throat loudly. I turned around in his direction. He was standing in the doorway; his thumbs stuck in his trouser pockets. He was smiling again, but at the same time he looked **impatient**, like somebody who can't wait until his aquarium has been put together.

»Yes?« he said. »But?«

»Well, I guess she can't fall in love with you because then she'd have to think about Dad.«

»Oh – I see.« Now he wasn't smiling anymore. He looked at me as though he'd just got a bad mark in a test. »I, um, I thought you lived alone?«

»We do. Dad has been dead for a long time.«

And now he was looking at me as though the teacher had just given him the wrong test back and he'd got ten out of ten after all. His face was very tanned, as if he'd spent the last few days in the sun. The only pale bit was the little scar on his chin.

»I'm very sorry for your loss.« His voice was suddenly so warm, I had the feeling the whole **wintry** room around me was **thawing**. »I'm very sorry for both of you!«

---

impatient – ungeduldig

wintry – frostig

to thaw – auftauen

»He died on a stormy day,« my voice said all by itself. »It was in autumn. Dad wanted –«

There was a noise like a mobile phone. It had a cool ring tone. It sounded like a mouse running over the keys of a piano.

»I'm sorry!« Mr Lake lifted one finger. »Don't run away, OK? I've been waiting for this call. It won't take long.« He turned round and ran out of the room. The noise stopped.

Frederico, I thought, you must be mad! I had been about to tell Mr Lake my biggest secret, and I wasn't even friends with him. How had he managed to make me do that? When he came back, I'd tell him I was sorry but I had to go.

He had disappeared into the room diagonally across from where I was. I stretched out my neck – it was the kitchen. He was speaking into his mobile in a muffled voice. I didn't understand a word, and before I could creep into the corridor to hear better, the phone call was already over. I drew my head back and looked casual.

»I'm afraid I have to go,« Mr Lake said, when he came back. He still looked nice, but he was acting all businesslike. He had a brown leather jacket in his hand. »But I've got a suggestion«, he said, as he slipped it on. »Why don't you come back tomorrow in the late afternoon, then I'll have a bit more time for you. And for your story. Agreed?«

»I don't know if –«

»If you'd rather not tell me, you don't have to. But the invitation stands, OK?« He pointed to the door and tried to smile, but couldn't hide his **agitation**. »And now off with you, you nosy child proddity!«

Mrs Dahling beamed at me like Halley's Comet when she saw me standing in front of her door unexpectedly and suddenly I realised that she had more grey days than she would like. For the first time I asked myself why she didn't have any children of her own.

»Mum has gone away,« I said as I she let me in. »She won't be back until the day after tomorrow at the earliest.«

»Where's she gone again?«

»To see her brother at the bottom and left. He's got cancer.«

»How terrible!« Mrs Dahling pushed the door shut and turned around with a look of shock on her face. »Where?«

»At the bottom and left.«

»I know that. I meant which part of the body?«

»Oh … no idea.«

Mrs Dahling shook her head sadly. »It's always the wrong person that gets it.«

»Who'd be the right one, then?«

»That caretaker,« she said, without batting an eyelid.

---

agitation – Aufregung

»What's up with him?«

»I had words with him as I came in. The door to the backyard has been sticking for weeks, you've probably noticed.« She was so cross she didn't even wait for me to nod. »You can barely get it open when you take the rubbish out; it's getting worse by the day! But do you think that walking bottle of whisky has done anything about it?«

I shrugged my shoulders and followed her past the pictures of laughing clowns into the kitchen. »At least cancer isn't catching,« I said to get her off the subject. If she carried on complaining, she might forget about the canapés.

»Did you think it was?« she asked over her shoulder.

»Of course not! I just thought you might not know that.«

Unlike stupid Mr Marrak, Mrs Dahling obviously didn't think it was too bad that Mum had left me by myself. She didn't mention it in any case and instead she finally got on to food.

»I was just about to make myself something to eat. Have you eaten already?«

»Granola, this afternoon.«

»Good, then we'll have some canapés.«

About time!

She opened the fridge to get the cheese, cucumbers and tomatoes. »By the way, it just so happens that I've bought a new film.«

I leaned against the table. »Is it a thriller?«

»A romance. *Pretty Woman.* Have you heard of it?«

»No. What's it about?«

»It's about a call girl who falls in love with a rich man.«

»What's a call girl?«

»Well.« Mrs Dahling turned back to the fridge and began **rummaging** through it. »What on earth did I do with the butter?«

»It's next to the mustard. What's a call girl? Or don't you know?«

»No, well, I do, but ...« Her shoulders shrugged forwards as though she was trying to fold herself in half. She turned around holding the butter in one hand and looked at me thoughtfully.

»Oh well, you're probably old enough.«

»Old enough for what?«

»Old enough to find out about certain things.« She put the butter on the table. »Well, a call girl is a woman whose job it is to make sure that men enjoy themselves.«

»Like Mum?«

»No. No, no, no!« She shook her head.

»Your mum *works* in a club where call girls meet men! She makes sure that all the men behave themselves and that they, well ... that they have enough to drink when they get thirsty.«

»She *manages* the club!« I said proudly. »She's in charge of the business. She decides which drinks to buy and things like that.«

---

to rummage – durchstöbern

»And things like that, yes,« said Mrs Dahling with a sigh. She took some bread out of the cupboard. »Now, let me make the food. Have a seat in the living room and turn on the **goggle box**. Then you can tell me what's going on in the world while we're eating.«

She was talking about politics. I would rather have carried on watching her.

»I won't remember.«

»Yes, you will. You've got a fantastic memory; don't let anybody tell you any different.«

»But I don't understand politics.«

»If they sent everybody who didn't understand politics to that special school of yours, they'd have an **overcrowding** problem.«

»It's not *my* special school!« I grumbled.

She waggled the bread knife in front of my nose. »Off you go, shoo, shoo! I don't like people getting under my feet in the kitchen.«

I went into the living room grumpily. I flopped onto the sofa, grabbed the remote control and switched on the giant goggle box. The telly is always switched to the local channel so that Mrs Dahling never misses her beloved Ulf Brauscher. Before the picture came on, a woman's voice could be heard.

---

goggle box – Flimmerkiste (ugs. für Fernseher)

to overcrowd – überfüllen

»– who has been terrorising Berlin for three months, has, it has just been announced, kidnapped his sixth victim. Our special edition will fill you in on the latest developments – in a case that is surprisingly different from its ***predecessors****!«*

You could see the woman reporter now, she was one of Ulf Brauscher's colleagues. Now and again they took turns doing the news from Berlin. The woman was trying to look concerned because there was a child involved. I didn't believe her, though. Grown-ups always look concerned on television when there's a child involved in a crime, and then in the supermarket they shove their shopping baskets into your back or very nearly push you into the freezer compartment if you get in their way.

But it was exciting all the same. The newsreader explained that it was unusual for the kidnapper to have released a child just last Saturday only to have snatched another one straight away. She was right. It was pretty quick. Maybe Mr 2000 had been afraid he wouldn't be able to get any kids over the summer because everybody would be away on holiday.

A map of Berlin came up on the screen. One part of town after another was highlighted in turn: Wedding, Charlottenburg, Kreuzberg and Tempelhof, Lichtenberg.

»There appears to be no pattern to the kidnappings. The police are assuming that Mr 2000 drives around ***aimlessly****, luring children into his vehicle when a suitable opportunity presents itself.«*

---

predecessor – Vorgänger

aimlessly – ziellos

Next up on the screen was Schöneberg. It had to be where the latest victim was from. The other parts of town weren't shown but six red dots flashed on the map to show where the kidnaps had taken place.

»Well,« Mrs Dahling called out from the kitchen. »Any news?«

»The ALDI kidnapper has **snatched** another kid!«

»Gracious me. Turn it up! Milk or juice?«

»Milk, please!«

I turned the volume up with the remote.

»For the first time in this series of kidnappings the father of the victim has turned to the police without paying the ransom money demanded.«

The six parts of town and the red dots turned into shaky camera shots. The upper right corner of the screen said *»Live«*. A youngish man who looked a bit scruffy came into view. There were so many microphones being held in front of his nose you could **scarcely** see his face in the crush. He kept blinking, because the flash of the cameras dazzled him. Reporters were calling out questions all around him.

»Why did you inform the police? The kidnapper usually threatens the kidnapped children with –«

»I don't have the money,« said the young man. »It's as simple as that.« And he added with a snort: »I had to go to

---

to snatch sb. – jmd. ergreifen

scarcely – kaum

the police because no bank in the world would have given me a loan. Not even for a kidnapped child.«

»What's a loan?« I called out to the kitchen.

»Money that you borrow from somebody for a while,« Mrs Dahling called back. »You have to pay more back later than you borrowed in the first place.«

I was just about to ask her if she wanted to borrow some money from me, but at that very moment the television showed a photo of the latest victim and my heart almost stopped.

The child was a boy.

The boy was Oskar.

He wasn't wearing his helmet but I recognised him immediately. Nobody has green eyes like Oskar and nobody has teeth that big. It could very well be that nobody has **sticky out ears** like that either. They stood out almost horizontally from Oskar's head. You could easily place a small glass containing a cold drink on each one.

»As the father of the boy explained, his seven-year-old son left home at around nine o'clock to visit a friend. But little Oskar never arrived.«

I barely understood what the newsreader was saying. There was a strange **buzzing** in my ears. Now Oskar's dad was surrounded by reporters again.

---

sticky out ears – Segelohren

to buzz – summen

»I don't know why he went out without his helmet. Normally he never leaves the house without his helmet! We live in a big city. Our streets are dangerous. I was always telling him that.«

»Why didn't you accompany your son? Wasn't that **neglecting** your parental duty?«

»No comment.«

»Did you know *who* Oskar was going to visit? Are you sure that the friend he was allegedly going to visit actually exists?«

»No comment.«

»At ten-thirty this morning Oskar's father, who is a single parent, received a call from the kidnapper. That too is unusual: up until now the kidnapper has always contacted the parents of his victims by letter. The kidnapper's demand, however, is the same as always: two thousand Euros. A meeting place for the handover of the ransom money has not yet been agreed.«

The buzzing in my ears grew less. Two thousand euros, I thought, two thousand Euros. Oskar's father obviously didn't have any rich friends or relatives who could lend him that much money. He didn't have a wife either. And Oskar almost certainly did not have a piggy bank. For somebody who was so afraid, that really wasn't very sensible. Even I had started saving up for my own kidnapping.

I jumped when Mrs Dahling turned up like a ghost and put the plate with the canapés down on the table. I hadn't

---

to neglect – vernachlässigen

heard her coming into the living room. She plumped up the soft cushion with the **tassels** that she always puts behind her back and sat down next to me on the sofa.

»Maybe they'll catch the swine now!« she snorted. »Maybe somebody saw the boy this morning and will remember.«

She leaned back on the cushion, stuck a canapé in her mouth and chewed it. Liver paté with cucumber. I sneaked a glance at her. She would probably believe me if I said that I not only knew Oskar but that he'd been on the way to see me this morning. And because she'd believe me, she'd drag me to the police so they could question me. Where did I know Oskar from and for how long had I known him and when had we seen each other last and at what point had we arranged to meet and at what time? What had we talked about? Had Oskar mentioned anything that would suggest he knew his kidnapper? The police would take me apart the way Miss Marple treated her **suspects**. The lottery machine would go crazy.

I'd die of embarrassment.

On the telly they were now showing the picture of the first kidnapped child. I knew what was coming next; they'd done it a thousand times already: they'd show one kid after another. Sad music was playing as though the victims had all been through a shredder instead of coming back in one piece.

---

tassel – Quaste

suspect – Verdächtiger

»Now they're just trying to make us cry,« said Mrs Dahling. »I'd better put the film on. What did I do with it? Oh yes, I think it's in my handbag.«

She pushed herself up from the sofa and disappeared into the hall. I carried on staring at the screen, dazed. My friend Oskar was the latest kidnap victim and he didn't even have a mum to worry about him! She was probably dead or something like that. I couldn't believe it. I should have been afraid for Oskar or felt sorry for him, but as the pictures of the kidnapped children were being shown, I felt like a bowl that had been completely licked clean of cake mix.

When the second victim popped up, I looked more closely. They'd got a new photo of Sophia. Her parents finally seemed to have realised that the TV kept showing a terrible picture of their daughter and had given the evening news a better one. Sophia was standing in a playground next to a **rocking horse** on springs. The photo must have been taken in the playground in front of her primary school, because in the background you could see a big building with colourful pictures stuck to the windows, probably from the inside.

Unlike the old, blurry photo, this one was really clear. Sophia didn't look much prettier on it than she usually did, but she did look much nicer. She was smiling. Her hair was washed and she was no longer wearing the wrinkled pink T-shirt with the big, fat strawberry stain on the chest, but an ironed, light blue one instead. However …

---

rocking horse – Schaukelpferd

I leaned forward. It was hard to believe, but Sophia had stained her light blue T-shirt in almost exactly the same place! The camera zoomed in on the picture. And for the second time that evening my heart stood still. It wasn't a stain, I could see that now.

It was a small, bright red aeroplane with a broken-off wing.

WEDNESDAY

LOOKING FOR SOPHIA

Dear Mum,

I have left the computer on on purpose so that you'll find my diary right away when you come home. I don't want you to worry, but I have to help Oskar. The boy with the blue helmet. If something happens to me, you can break into my Reichstag to pay for the funeral. If Uncle Christian has died, you can put me in his coffin. If I'm dead, I won't mind. With deepest sympathy!

Love

Rico

p.s. Mr Lake will take care of you. He's very nice and has a beautiful living room, especially the ceiling. I love you!

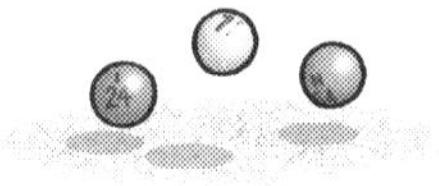

It was eight-thirty in the morning and the day was fresh and wet. I stood in front of Dieffe 93 and looked into a dirty **puddle** that the rain had left behind on the pavement the night before. Seeds from the trees with the peeling-off bark were raining into the puddle, hundreds and hundreds of them. They looked like tiny **parachutists**. Now and again a drop fell from the branches above me, splashed into the

---

puddle – Pfütze

parachutists – Fallschirmspringer

puddle and sent the seeds shooting over the water like little boats.

I was well equipped. Mum's map of Berlin was in my bag. I had the money that she'd left me too – twenty euros. And when I patted the pocket of my trousers, I could feel the red aeroplane that I had fished out of the rubbish bin.

One thing was clear: Sophia must have given Oskar the aeroplane as a present – this very aeroplane with the broken-off wing. I couldn't imagine that he'd stolen it.

But why had he visited Sophia in Tempelhof?

What had she told him?

Though on the one hand it was quite difficult to believe, on the other I couldn't help suspecting that Oskar had tried to track down Mr 2000 all by himself. I didn't know where he had got hold of this mad idea and why his search had brought him to Dieffe last Saturday. But he must have been following a **clue** that he had got from Sophia. A really important clue that Sophia had either not told the police or that nobody had believed when she had told them.

My head was spinning so much it hurt. Maybe Mr 2000 hadn't chosen Oskar, but had kidnapped him because Oskar had been on his trail. Had Oskar been planning to catch Mr 2000 by offering himself up as **bait**? And if that was the case, why hadn't Oskar let anybody in on his plan?

---

clue – Hinweis

bait – Köder

The thoughts were flying wildly round my head, like chickens **squawking** because they're being chased by somebody with a **meat cleaver**. The night before I had fallen asleep in the thinking chair from all the effort, but before I did I had the idea of looking for Sophia. Now, here I was, trying to set out to find Sophia but rooted to the spot, staring at this stupid puddle.

Oh God, oh God!

I'd never been out of my street by myself. I'd been with other people, though. Irina has a fast car, and on nice summer days Mum and I go for drives with her. We cruise from Alexanderplatz to the radio tower and back, past the Brandenburg Gate and then into Mitte, listening to cool Russian music. If we like the look of a street, then we get out and sit at a cool pavement café. The sun shines on Irina's golden ankle chain and on Mum's fingernails with their pink shimmer or whatever else is on them, and Mum and Irina drink champagne and laugh themselves silly, and I drink Coke and I'm happy that so many men think Mum is great. Everybody looks at her, but Mum never asks any of them if they'd like some of her champagne.

But getting round Berlin by myself is another matter. The very idea of setting off to find Sophia in Tempelhof without really knowing which way to go froze me to the pavement. I wasn't brave enough to open Mum's large map of the city.

---

to squawk – krächzen

meat cleaver – Fleischerbeil

All those lines and bright colours and then the tiny letters and all those funny symbols. Not for Rico! The map and the lottery balls in my head were made for each other.

What a great start.

I turned around as the door to the building opened behind me. Mr Kiesling isn't as good-looking as Mr Lake, but he's not much worse-looking. Mrs Dahling says he's always **neat as a pin**, and she's right. He wears extremely cool clothes and shoes and he has a huge collection of sunglasses. Mrs Dahling is always asking herself how he pays for all that stuff on his salary. Mr Kiesling also goes to the hairdresser's once a week, and he owns the coolest car in all of Dieffe, an old Porsche where you have to wind the windows down by hand. The car was right on the other side of the street. Mr Kiesling had the key in his hand as he came out of the door.

Sometimes, when you have a good idea, it's almost as though you can't breathe for a moment. Unfortunately everybody notices because of the colour of your face. Mr Kiesling could see it even through his dark glasses.

»Everything all right, Rico?« he said.

I forced myself to breathe in and nodded. We don't know each other that well. Mr Kiesling hadn't been all that impressed when I wanted to look at his flat, and when we meet in the stairway, we almost never talk.

»You're up early,« he said. »Aren't you on holiday?«

»I was waiting for you,« I said.

---

neat as a pin – wie aus dem Ei gepellt

He pushed up his sunglasses in surprise. »For me?«

»I'm going in your direction,« I said. The dental laboratory where he works is in Tempelhof where Sophia lives. I should have realised that a lot earlier.

»Tempelhof? What are you up to over there?«

»Visiting a girl.«

»Oh yeah?« He always looks a bit arrogant when he grins. »I thought evenings were for visiting girls.«

»Not a going-out-with kind of girl!« I said. I almost told him that I really like Jule, but it's none of his business. I don't ask him about his love life. »So will you take me with you?«

»Be my guest!« he said and pointed to the Porsche. »But if you get the car dirty, I'll throw you out right there and then!«

We crossed the street and he opened the **passenger door** for me. As soon as I was sitting in the car, I dug the *map* out of my rucksack, opened it and ran my finger over it. Mr Kiesling got in on the other side, put his seatbelt on and glanced at the map.

»What are you looking for?«

»The school.«

»Which school?«

»The one where I'm going to meet my friend in the playground.«

»I thought you wanted to go to Tempelhof. Why have you got the map open at Grunewald?«

---

passenger door – Beifahrertür

It was one of the few double pages in the map that didn't have many roads marked. Everything was nicely green because of all the trees, although up until a minute ago I'd thought they were fields. Most of the paths that were drawn in had very simple names, and the River Havel was flowing on one side, nicely blue. I stuck the map under Mr Kiesling's nose.

»Could you look for me? I'm a bit lost,« I admitted, **reluctantly**.

»Because of your learning difficulties, or what?«

I had to bite my lip to stay calm. The way he said it just like that, and the grin on his face! If I shouted at Mr Kiesling now, he'd never take me with him. It's annoying when people think you're totally stupid just because your brain works in a different way to theirs. The problem is that my brain sometimes behaves as though it's trying to drive a car without a **steering wheel**. I don't complain that other people think too fast or that somebody invented left and right and all the points of the compass and ovens with twenty-seven different settings for baking bread rolls.

»I'm not a child proddity on purpose, and anyway I'm only a little bit of one,« I said, angrily, and pointed at the map. »Sometimes I just don't know where front and back is and things like that.«

»Really?« said Mr Kiesling. »Well, welcome to the club.«

---

reluctantly – widerwillig

steering wheel – Lenkrad

»It's nothing to be ashamed of, is it?«

»I never said it was.«

»And I've got a really good memory.«

»All right, all right!« He put both his hands up in the air as though I was threatening him with a pistol. »I'm sorry if I offended you. So, what's the name of the school?«

I leaned back in my seat. »I've forgotten.«

He sighed impatiently. »Listen, kid, we won't get anywhere like this. There are God knows how many primary schools in Tempelhof, I can't possibly drive past all of them.«

I wrinkled my nose. Mr Kiesling rolled his eyes.

»All right then, listen. There's a school I drive past on my way to work. I'll **drop you off** there. After that you'll have to figure it out by yourself. I can't be late for work because of you.«

I opened my mouth to reply.

»No ifs or buts!« He put his key in the **ignition** and mumbled so I could hardly understand: »I had enough problems on Monday for taking the afternoon off.«

»What for?« I asked, interested. Monday was the day I'd seen him in the stairway with Mr Lake and Mr Marrak.

»That's of no interest to little boys.«

»Why not?«

»Because it's got something to do with big boys.«

---

to drop sb. off – jmd. absetzten

ignition – Zündschloss

He must think I've never seen men kissing and stuff like that. I pushed myself even lower into my seat. »Are we going then?«

»As soon as you've put your **seatbelt** on, kiddo.« Mr Kiesling pulled his sunglasses back over his eyes and turned the key. »And if you promise me that you'll keep your mouth shut while we're driving.«

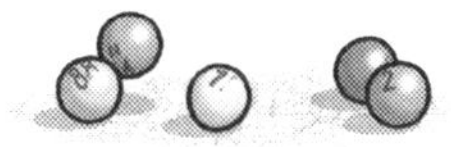

I was very lucky that the school where Mr Kiesling let me out turned out to be the right one. Who knows what would have happened otherwise? I recognised the building right away from the new picture of Sophia on telly – the red bricks, the decorated windows; I even discovered the rocking horse on springs on the playground.

Behind me Mr Kiesling hit the **accelerator** and drove off with screeching **tyres**. I watched him for a while. Riding in the Porsche was brilliant! It didn't feel like driving; it felt like floating over the ground. The motor had **purred** like a happy cat, and Mr Kiesling had barely needed to turn the

seatbelt – Sicherheitsgurt
accelerator – Gaspedal
tyres – Reifen
to purr – schnurren

steering wheel. To be fair, that was because we had driven straight ahead for quite a while in the beginning, had only turned off once at a crossroads and then driven straight ahead again for ages. But it had been cool. Mr Kiesling had put his foot on the accelerator impatiently at every traffic light. The engine had revved up and everybody had looked at us. It was great!

It was only the last bit that was difficult: a little turn here and a little turn there, more crossroads, more traffic lights, and in between the lottery balls in my head banging into each other and saying the same thing over and over again: *You'll never find the way home, you'll never find the way home …*

We'd see about that!

I looked around. The playground in front of the school, which had some green bushes around it, was empty. Almost nobody goes to a playground at nine-thirty in the morning in the holidays. I was expecting that, but I knew that the longer I stayed here, the more chance I had of meeting somebody who could help me – a child that went to school here too and knew Sophia, the famous girl who had been kidnapped.

I stomped around a bit. The seats on the swings **glistened** with water. The sand in the sandpit was dark grey and sticky. Fat drops of rain clung to the metal of the climbing frame. Off to one side, on the way to the school building, there was a bench. Two boys were sitting on the back of it.

---

to glisten – flimmern

One of them had blonde, stubbly hair and was about as tall as Oskar. The other one had untidy brown hair, was quite a bit larger than I was and was talking to **stubblehead**. If he was used to younger kids, he probably wouldn't tell me to get lost if he didn't like the look of me.

I wandered over to the two of them. The big one was so busy talking that he didn't notice me until I was only two metres away. The little one had been watching me the whole time without moving a centimetre.

»What?« said the big one, as I stood in front of them. He didn't look mean or unfriendly, just annoyed at being disturbed.

»Do you know your way around here?« I asked him.

»Why?«

»I'm looking for someone who lives nearby.«

I was only guessing, but most kids don't live far away from their school. Sophia might only be a few streets away in her room, arranging her T-shirts.

The big one didn't answer.

»She's called Sophia and she goes to this school,« I went on. »I don't know her surname. She's the girl who was **abducted** by the ALDI kidnapper.«

He nodded as though people asked him about Sophia every day. »And if I do know where she lives?«

»You can tell me.«

---

stubblehead – Stoppelkopf

to abduct sb. – jmd. entführen

»What's your name?«

»My name's Rico.«

»Felix.«

»No, Rico.« Hadn't he heard me?

»*I'm* Felix. So, what do you want from Sophia?«

»She's my friend.«

»You don't know her surname and you don't know where she lives?« He laughed quietly. »You can't be friends.«

»I can't remember addresses and things like that. I'm a child proddity.«

Felix screwed his eyes together. He didn't understand the word. It only took a second for me to battle with myself and say that other thing I hated. »I have learning difficulties. But only sometimes,« I added quickly.

The blonde stubblehead kept on looking at me without making a sound. He probably wasn't even breathing. He had light blue, somehow watery eyes that looked as though ladybirds could have a bath in them. I found him a bit freaky.

»So, assuming you *are* nice, just a bit weird,« said Felix, »why should I tell you anything about Sophia?«

»Do you know where she lives, then?«

»I'm in the same class as her brother. He's a complete idiot.« He thought for a second. »Maybe anyone would turn into a complete idiot if they had to share a room with their little sister. I know I'd go crazy. But maybe Tobias is a child proddity too.«

»Who's Tobias?«

»Sophia's brother, you **brainwarp**!«

That was it! First Mr Kiesling and now Felix too. For the second time that morning I had to swallow my anger to carry on. If I ever saw Oskar again, he owed me more than just a walk by the canal followed by an ice cream; a lot more.

»If you'd been here five minutes earlier, you'd have bumped into Tobias. His mum sent him shopping.« He giggled quietly and pointed with one hand over his shoulder. »Over to ALDI.«

»I just want to ask Sophia something,« I said.

»What?«

He wouldn't take me to her unless I told him. He didn't say so, but I could see it on his face.

I took a deep breath. »The boy who was kidnapped yesterday ...«

»What about him?«

»Sophia knows him. And I thought I'd ask her –«

»If she put him on to Mr 2000? You're crazy!« He let out a loud laugh. Then he turned serious again. »What do you think she can tell you? Stuff that she didn't tell the police?«

»Something like that,« I murmured.

»Because she'd rather trust a kid than a grown up?«

I nodded. That had been my idea, and Oskar must have had the same one.

»Well then.«

---

brainwarp – Hirnbremse

Felix suddenly swung himself off the bench. Stubblehead did the same thing.

»You know what you're getting yourself into, don't you?« said Felix, as we left the playground. »Mr 2000 himself, the most cunning kidnapper of all time! If he catches you, the first thing he'll do is cut your ears off.«

»Says who?«

»Says me. They always cut your ears off first.«

I hadn't known that.

»Then a hand! And then, if he still hasn't got his money, the arm it belongs to. He has to leave the other arm on to start with so that you can still write your parents a **begging letter**, see? That's why he'll take your legs off next.«

»You're making it up.«

He shook his head and his brown hair got even more untidy. »I want to write books one day, and writers make things up all the time, you know?«

»I only read comics.«

»Well, they're made up from start to finish.«

It was difficult to keep up with him. He took huge steps. »And have you written anything yet?«

»Quite a lot.«

»Is it good?«

»You'll have to ask Sven.«

»Who's Sven?«

»Who do you think?«

---

begging letter – Bettelbrief

Stubblehead still didn't say a word. He had to take twice as many steps as Felix, but he trotted along next to him as though he was fastened to him by an invisible rope.

»I tell him all my new ideas,« said Felix. »If he thinks a story's good, I write it down. And not before.«

That was what he'd been doing when I arrived. He'd been telling Sven his latest story. I raised a hand and waved at Sven. »Hello, Sven.«

No reply. Sven didn't even look at me.

»He can't hear you,« said Felix. »He can't speak either. He's deaf and dumb.«

»You don't say deaf and dumb. It's called **hearing impaired**.« I knew that from school.

»Whatever.« Felix walked even more quickly, looking straight ahead. »He's the only person who listens to me.«

The flats where Sophia lived were in between a lot of other flats that all looked the same. They had no balconies, smooth front walls and were painted brown. The wooden window frames looked as though they had once been white.

---

hearing impaired – hörgeschädigt

Felix showed me which bell to ring before leaving for who knows where with Sven **in tow**. I watched the two of them go. How crazy do you have to be to tell your stories to somebody who's hearing impaired? And how crazy do you have to be to listen to somebody you can't hear? But Felix and Sven didn't seem embarrassed. They were friends. For them it was the most normal thing in the world. And that made me feel a lot better.

But not for long.

When Sophia's mum opened the door, a wave of grey day washed over me. There was even a grey smell. Sophia's mum didn't look like a mum who was interested in which children were in her kid's class at school. Luckily for me. She was wearing a **grubby** dressing gown and waved me into the flat before I'd finished saying my lines.

»Good morning. I'm a friend of Tobias's and –«

»He's gone shopping.« I stood in front of her in a gloomy hallway. She pointed past my shoulder with one hand. In the other she was holding a smoking cigarette. »He'll be back soon. You can wait in his room.«

I looked closely at her fingernails. They were splintered and painted pink. With no stickers. My mum would never go out in public with nails like that. And she always brushed her hair right after cleaning her teeth.

---

to tow – abschleppen

grubby – schmuddelig

Sophia's mum shuffled back into the living room. I could see a flat-screen TV through the open door. It was even bigger than Mrs Dahling's and had to be brand new, because it was the only thing in the entire flat that gleamed. I'd already been able to hear it quite clearly outside the front door on the stairs. Here, in the flat, it was annoyingly loud. Two neighbours were arguing on a chat show. One of them had peed over the other one's **garden fence** while drunk and his neighbour's squash plant had died.

> SQUASH: Juice in a bottle that you mix with water to make a drink. No idea why anybody would pee on a bottle of squash or why you would plant one in the garden.

At the end of the hall there were two more rooms. On one of the doors there were colourful pictures and a Barbie poster. I knocked quietly and went in. If Sophia wasn't at home, I'd clear off right away without telling anybody.

The room was the biggest mess I'd ever seen. Toys, clothes, comics, school stuff, CD cases and computer games were scattered all over the floor. There were empty and half-empty bottles, used plates and cups lying all over the place. You would need days to clear a path through all that mess

---

garden fence – Gartenzaun

and get outside into the hall. And over everything lay a sad, grey cloud of dust, as though a **hoover bag** had exploded here fifty years ago.

The top of Sophia's body stuck out of all the chaos like a sinking ship. She was just standing there, in the middle of the room, as though she'd been waiting for someone for a long time or was practising for a competition in falling asleep while standing up.

»Hi!« I said.

Her thin, colourless eyebrows made a frown. Her gaze was cloudy, as though her eyes were trying not to be noticed in this grey room. Behind her a **bunkbed** stuck up out of the rubbish like another sinking ship. She must get quite tired fighting her way into bed each night. I pulled the red aeroplane out of my trouser pocket. Suddenly Sophia's eyes lit up.

»I got it from Oskar, and he got it from you,« I said quickly. I didn't have a lot of time. Tobias could come back from his shopping trip at any moment and tell his mum he'd never seen me before in his life.

She stared at the aeroplane. Her eyes filled with tears.

»He's in great danger – you know that, don't you?« I asked.

For a moment I was afraid she hadn't heard about Oskar's kidnapping, but then she nodded. I would have been sur-

---

hoover bag – Staubsaugerbeutel

bunkbed – Hochbett

prised if she hadn't; the telly seemed to be on here all day. You could hear the **bickering** of the angry neighbours on the chat show even in here.

»You told Oskar something, didn't you?« I said, carefully. »Something that you didn't tell the police because the kidnapper told you something terrible would happen if you did. Am I right?«

Finally, she opened her mouth. Her voice was squeaky, like a bird that's just left the nest but doesn't trust itself to fly.

»The jingle-jangle man said that if I grassed on him, he'd come and get Jannek and kill him.«

»Jannek?«

She pointed to a sticky desk that was so full you couldn't even have written a shopping list on it. A television stood next to a computer screen. There was a round goldfish bowl behind a greasy, crumpled McDonald's wrapper. Something was swimming around in it.

»That's Jannek. He's sick. He's got something on his fins.«

Well really, if that wasn't the saddest thing in the world! Mr 2000 must have asked Sophia who she loved best so that he could **blackmail** her into keeping quiet. And Sophia must have said her goldfish!

I stared at the round bowl and Jannek stared back. He waggled two colourless, strangely frayed fins. I felt queasy. Maybe the germs lurking between the piles of rubbish were

---

to bicker – streiten

to blackmail – erpressen

responsible for the illness. Maybe they were jumping **germs**. I breathed in very carefully and concentrated on Sophia again.

»Why do you call the kidnapper the jingle-jangle man?«

She shook her head slowly but stubbornly.

»You can tell me. I won't tell anybody.«

»That's what Oskar said!« she said in an unexpectedly loud voice. »And now he's locked up in the green room!«

»Which green room?«

There was no reply.

»Sophia, Oskar is my friend,« I insisted. »I want to help him, but I can't do that unless you help me!«

She glared at me suspiciously.

She clenched her little hands into fists.

Her narrow lips got even thinner.

There was nothing to be done. She wasn't going to tell me anything else. I held out the red aeroplane. She took it slowly as though it was the most precious thing she'd ever been given. She stroked the broken wing with a clumsy finger.

»He said he liked me,« she said quietly.

»He does. He wore the aeroplane all the time. But then he must have lost it. Maybe when he was kidnapped.«

She looked up at me, very stubborn again. »I was expensive,« she said.

»Yes, I know.«

---

germ – Bazille

»But Mum got money for the interviews.«

I nodded. That explained the new TV. Its noise followed me out of the door as I left the sad flat where the grey days had made themselves at home.

Now I had to get home. Back outside, things started to feel a little scary. The large buildings all around me seemed to be creeping closer together and bending down towards me. The dirty white windows stared at me like a thousand eyes. I rummaged around madly in my rucksack for the map, opened it, looked inside and closed it again immediately. I'll bet people have gone crazy trying to read maps.

I'd have to go about it some other way. If I found an underground station, surely I'd manage. I just had to catch a train that was going to Kottbusser Tor; the rest would be easy. I can always see the entrance to Kottie when I'm at the Doyum kebab house. From there to home it was just the other way around.

There was a shop on the other side of the street. I could ask the way there. There was no **zebra crossing** in sight, but there was hardly any traffic.

---

zebra crossing – Zebrastreifen

Every year almost forty thousand children in Germany die in accidents, I could hear Oskar saying. *Twenty-five per cent are pedestrians.*

That must be more than a hundred, I guessed. I stretched one arm out just to be on the safe side, one hand pointing forward like an arrow, and ran right across the street with my eyes screwed tightly shut.

No screeching of brakes, no **honking**. Everything went smoothly.

No accident.

In front of the shop there were all kinds of newspaper stands full of bold headlines about Oskar's kidnapping. In one newspaper there was a map similar to the one I'd seen yesterday on television, with six red dots on it showing the location of each kidnapping. Underneath it said: *The Pattern of Terror!* And in smaller letters: *Parents' Panic – Could YOUR Child Be Next?*

Either the woman at the counter hadn't read the newspapers or else she didn't care if kids ran around without their parents. Whichever it was, she didn't ask any questions when I asked her how to get to the nearest underground station.

I couldn't remember the directions she gave me. There was so much *turn left here* and *go right there* and then *left again* that I got really dizzy. But I said thank you in a friendly voice. It wasn't her fault that I could only walk in a straight line.

---

to honk – hupen

Back on the street I **trudged** along. There was bound to be a bus stop somewhere or something similar, or I might find the underground station.

Then I saw the line of taxis. I trotted up to them in relief. I had never taken a taxi in my life and I had no idea if Mum's twenty euros would get me all the way to Dieffe, but it would be money well spent. At least Mum would get me back and wouldn't have to pick me up in the Alps or from the Pacific Ocean because I'd got lost.

I crawled onto the back seat of the first car and closed the door behind me. The driver had a roll of fat at the back of his neck. He turned around to look at me.

»What's all this about?« he barked at me.

»What's all what about?«

»What's a garden gnome like you doing alone on the street? Where are your parents?«

I had pretty much had enough.

»I've got to go home, but I can't find the way,« I said. »And before you ask why – I'm a child proddity!«

»Oh yeah? That's what all you brats are these days!«

I didn't want to talk back. I just wanted to be at home in the thinking chair. A jingle-jangle man and a green room … great! I hadn't the **faintest idea** what either of them meant. I had travelled all that way to see Sophia for nothing. Tears came to my eyes, but the taxi driver wasn't one bit sympa-

---

to trudge – trotten

faintest idea – geringste Ahnung

thetic. He was still looking me up and down. I tried Oskar's trick and stared back at him, but it didn't work.

»I'll ask you again. Where are your parents?«

He wouldn't drive off until I'd given him some kind of answer that satisfied him. Honestly, how annoying! He knew his way around the city and didn't know what it felt like when you have problems with directions and your only friend has been kidnapped from under your nose.

»I was with a friend from school,« I said finally. »My mum phoned. My dad is dead and I have to go home straight away. She told me to take a taxi.«

It was a pretty **desperate** thing to say, but it worked. I finally started to cry and the taxi driver looked all worried. He turned around, started the car and drove off. He didn't say another word until he'd dropped me off in front of my building in Dieffe, and when he took thirteen euros forty off me, he almost looked as though he felt bad about it.

---

desperate – verzweifelt

WEDNESDAY AGAIN

SHADOWIER SHADOWS

Bad things take all your energy and make your legs shake. By midday I had typed everything that had happened into my diary. Now I was sitting in the thinking chair, staring out of the window and thinking about Felix telling his stories with no one to listen to them, about silent Sven with his ladybird-bath eyes and about Sophia, surrounded by all those grey days. I thought about Oskar, locked up somewhere, really frightened even though he's so clever. Then I thought about me, sitting around here because I'm a child proddity and don't know what to do next. Somebody who is cleverer than I am would have been able to get more clues out of Sophia.

> DEPRESSION: Grey days. Mum called it that once when we were talking about Mrs Dahling. Depression is when all your feelings are in a wheelchair. They don't have arms anymore and sadly there's no one to push them either. The tyres are probably flat too. It makes you very tired.

I crept into my room and lay down on the bed. Now and then I squinted through the window at the cracked front of the building behind ours, which looked less scary during the day than it did in the evening and at night when the shadowier shadows came. I could still be a little bit happy and proud, I thought, because I'd been brave enough to go to Tempelhof alone and had survived.

My eyes closed all by themselves. Last night I slept badly and not long enough. At one point I jumped up because I thought the phone had rung, but the flat was quiet. Then I dozed off again. After yesterday's rainy day and the dull morning, the sun was shining brightly. It must have been really hot outside.

I dreamt that Oskar was standing in front of me on the RBs' roof terrace. He had just proved his courage by leaning over the railing and looking down into the backyard. Then he looked at me and I really wanted to know if he was my friend. I heard myself asking if he would come again tomorrow. I saw Oskar scratching his arm. Fingering his aeroplane badge. Chewing on his lower lip with his large teeth, before he said: *Actually, I've got plans for tomorrow. They could take all day.*

I woke up with a start as though somebody had hit me over the head, only it didn't hurt. Something was wrong with the dream. Or something was wrong with my memory. I could almost reach it with both hands, but when I grasped for it …

Keep calm, Rico, don't get excited! I closed my eyes and called up the images again. Sun on the roof terrace. Oskar leaning against the railing that looks out onto the backyard, rock, rock, rocking. Scratching his arm. Fingering the aeroplane that I found the next day in the rubbish bin, the small red aeroplane, the aeroplane –

– that up until now I had thought had fallen off his shirt into the yard while he was swinging on the railing!

I sat up in bed with such a start that I got dizzy. My memory was wrong! Oskar had still been wearing Sophia's plane when he stepped back from the railing on the RBs' roof terrace. Which could only mean …

»He came back again later on,« I whispered.

But when? After we had said goodbye on Monday, I had seen Oskar leaving the building from the living-room window. I had fun counting the number of steps he took from the stairs down to the street, to find out if he was as fast as me. Oskar had been faster than my counting. On Monday he definitely hadn't been in the backyard, unless he'd come back later and had rung somebody else's doorbell – very unlikely. And on Tuesday, yesterday morning, he had already been kidnapped, probably while he was on his way to see me.

And that could only mean …

It could only mean …

I had no idea what it could, should or had to mean. Once again I could feel my heart beating and a thousand birds fluttering through my head. I pressed both my hands against my ears. I stared out of the window towards the building behind us, wondering what to do. I must have been asleep for ages because it was going dark outside. My stomach was rumbling with hunger. It wouldn't have taken much and I'd have cried for the second time that day.

But I didn't want to cry. I had to talk to somebody. Sometimes, when you tell people something that's got you really confused, you're less confused afterwards.

And I knew exactly who I could talk to.

»I was wondering if you'd remember my invitation and stop by this afternoon,« Mr Lake said. »We'd agreed to meet, but …«

I hadn't forgotten. Most of all I remembered the warm feeling that flooded through me when I'd been about to tell him the story of my dead dad. How Mr Lake had looked at me and how his wintry living room had seemed to thaw around me. I felt like a small boat on top of high waves out in the open sea, and Mr Lake was my port in the storm.

»… but I had the impression you might have scared yourself with your own bravery.«

»What's bravery?«

»It's when you are scared of something but you still face up to it.«

I nodded. I'd learned a new word, but I had no idea how Mr Lake had begun the sentence. If I admitted that to him, he'd probably think I was an idiot again, and it was important – at that moment it was the most important thing in the world – that Mr Lake liked me. Mr Lake had to help me find Oskar.

I sat in his white living room on his white sofa. I was careful not to look up at the beautiful ceiling so I didn't get thinking about the aquarium and all that. There was a Coke on the table in front of me. I thought about asking Mr Lake for canapés, but he might have thought that was rude. He stood there with the cool scar on his chin, smiling that fantastic actor smile of his, looking down at me.

»Has your mum been in touch?« he said.

»I think she tried. The phone rang, but I was asleep.«

I sipped my Coke carefully. You have to be careful with Coke. I've heard that if you drink too much of it, it burns holes in your stomach from the inside, and then the Coke **glugs** right the way through you, and when you're at the cheese counter at the supermarket, you suddenly notice brown stuff running out of your nose.

»Don't you have a mobile phone?« said Mr Lake.

»Nah. Too expensive.« To be honest I wouldn't know who to call apart from Mum. I suppose I could always call one of those funny numbers on the television, the ones where you can get French recipes or Brazilian lottery numbers or find out how high the water level is in some river in Russia, but who really wants to know any of that? It's a complete waste of money, Mum always says.

---

to glug – gluckern

You'd think Mr Lake's mobile phone must have heard him, because it suddenly started to jingle, just like it did the last time I'd visited. Mr Lake rolled his eyes in annoyance. »It seems to be our **fate**,« he murmured. »Whenever we're about to have a chat ...«

He pulled his mobile out of his trouser pocket, glanced at it and suddenly looked as though he'd much rather be talking to the caller than to me.

»Answer it if you want to,« I said, nicely. As long as he didn't rush out of the flat again right after the call ...

Mr Lake's lips moved as though they were saying *Excuse me*, and the next minute he disappeared from the living room.

I put my Coke down and looked around. Nothing had changed; everything looked exactly the same as yesterday. Even the empty glass was still standing untouched on top of the BILD newspaper. The water stain had dried in right above Cindy the nail technician's boobs. I wrinkled my nose, reached for the glass and placed it a little bit further away from me. What a mess! Mr Lake would have to get used to being a bit tidier. Chaos can really mess you up, especially if it has boobs.

As I lifted the newspaper to fold it up, I saw a small, open map of Berlin underneath it. There was a **felt-tip pen** next to it. A few places on the map had been marked in red. The

---

fate – Schicksal

felt-tip pen – Filzstift

marks made the pattern that was in all the Berlin newspapers that day.

Six red marks.

Six kidnappings.

I stared in horror at the red **squiggles**. There's a saying that some people can't put two and two together. Which might be true, although it's not my fault that I always get four.

At least almost always.

Winter swept over the living room again. I felt as cold as if somebody had turned my heart into a giant ice cube. Oskar's kidnapping hadn't been announced until the special edition of the news yesterday evening. But the six red marks on the map in front of me had already been drawn in yesterday afternoon when I'd visited Mr Lake. Mr Lake had known about Oskar's kidnapping hours before the rest of the world had found out about it! And there was something else …

The jingle-jangle man said if I grass on him …

I'd just heard the jingle on Mr Lake's mobile again – mice running over the keyboard of a piano.

Cold and colder. Ice cold.

As I got up from the sofa as carefully as possible, I almost thought I heard a snap, like when you break an **icicle** off a gutter. I crept to the door of the living room and peered

---

squiggles – Schnörkel

icicle – Eiszapfen

into the hall. I could hear Mr Lake talking quietly but angrily in his kitchen, and what I heard made all the hairs on my arms stand up on end.

»... only got the two thousand euros together after you had gone public with your tragic story to try and persuade some bank or other to give you a free loan! You don't quite seem to understand what an impossible position you've put me into by doing that! I'm sorry, but the boy's life isn't worth a bean now ...«

A heartbeat later I was outside in the stairway. Another heartbeat later it occurred to me that I hadn't pushed the newspaper back over the map. I whirled around, but it was too late. The door to Mr Lake's flat slammed shut with a thunderous KEZAM.

As if things weren't bad enough already.

Behind the door Mr Lake called out: »Rico? Rico!«

I sprinted off.

What people in thrillers always do wrong when they're being followed is run to exactly the place that's most dangerous. Not me.

In the time it took Mr Lake to work out what I had found out in his living room, I didn't run downstairs to our flat, where the two-faced kidnapper would look for me right away. Instead I **scampered up** a floor as fast and as quietly as I could. I always had the RBs' key in my trouser pocket so that I didn't lose it. Now I let myself into the roof-top flat and pulled the door to behind me, so that it was only open a tiny crack, and listened.

Not a moment too soon. A door opened on the stairs and then Mr Lake's voice called: »Rico?«

I heard his footsteps going quickly downstairs to the second floor. Heard him ringing our bell. Heard him knocking on our door, then banging it hard.

»Rico?«

There was silence for a few seconds. He was thinking. He was arriving at the most obvious explanation; that I must have raced out of the building, who knows where, probably to the nearest police station to tell them I'd found the kidnapper. Finally, steps again, coming up the stairs. I held my breath. They stopped on the floor below me. As quietly as I could, I pressed the door shut and pressed my back against it. I waited. And thought.

Waiting was the easy part. What was I supposed to do now? I didn't want to go downstairs. Mr Lake was probably listening out for every noise in the building and would catch me on the fourth floor straight away. If I shouted out of a window, he'd be up here faster than anybody else. He looked like somebody who could easily break down a front door.

---

to scamper up – hochflitzen

Right, what were my other options? In the flat directly below me Mr Fitzke was probably **mooching around**, listening out for any noise – and almost certainly mean enough to hand me over to Mr Lake with an icy smile! He would ask only for my head, because he collected children's heads and played football with them in his stinky den, and the only thing missing from his collection was the head of a child proddity.

I couldn't go any further up either, apart from out onto the roof terrace. From there I could escape over the roofs of the next-door buildings – provided I didn't fall. If that happened, all I'd be able to do was wave to Mrs Dahling as I flew past and thank her for all the canapés, and that would be it.

SPLAT!

I could work my way round the partition onto Mr Marrak's roof terrace. With a bit of luck his terrace door would be open; it was a hot summer's day after all. But then? Mr Marrak was probably at his girlfriend's, taking her more washing or kissing her for a change. Then I'd be stuck in his flat instead of in here. And even if Mr Marrak was at home, he wouldn't believe me. I knew he couldn't stand me any more than Mr Kiesling or Mr Fitzke could. Suddenly I had the terrible feeling that all kinds of people only treated me nicely because they thought I was disabled. In reality I got on their nerves, but of course you can't say that to a **handi-**

---

to mooch around – herumlungern

capped person in case they start to cry. In any case, Mr Marrak would think I was being silly and – even worse – drag me off to say sorry to Mr Lake. Just so that everybody could have a good laugh at me. Mr Lake would wait until Mr Marrak had gone and then cut me into little strips, put them in a parcel and send them to Mum, while Oskar's strips were winging their way to his dad at the same time.

The simple ideas only come to you right at the end of lots of difficult thinking. My gaze wandered across the hall and landed on the telephone. That was the answer! Luckily the suspicious RBs hadn't hidden it in one of the locked rooms to stop me calling one of those expensive women with the big boobs from night-time television.

I went to the phone, picked it up and stared at it. I don't know Mum's mobile number off by heart. That's why Mum wrote the number down twice for me. One of the pieces of paper is stuck above our own telephone in the hallway, next to the mirror with the little fat **cherubs**. I put the other piece of paper in my pocket and then I lost it of course. Since then I've meant to write the number down again a thousand times, and I've forgotten to do it a thousand times.

And look where I AM now.

Then I grinned. There's one telephone number that I do know off by heart. It only has three numbers. Even some-

---

handicapped – beeinträchtigt, behindert

cherubs – Engel, Putten

one like me can learn it. Mum made me repeat it at breakfast for weeks on end: »Who do you call if you're in trouble and you can't reach me?«

I took a deep breath, **dialled** One, then One again, and then Zero, and listened hard. It took quite a long time for somebody to pick up. If Mr Lake had been after me with a knife, I thought, he would have sawn off my nose and both my ears in that time. Then, finally, as I was starting to think I'd dialled the wrong number –

»Emergency services,« a man's voice squawked into my ear. »How can I help?«

All at once everything was too fast for me. I hadn't thought about what I wanted to say. Now I was confused before I'd even had time to get confused.

»Hello?« I said, nervously.

»Emergency services. Speak up, please!«

»My … my name is Frederico Doretti,« I stammered. »I'm a child proddity. That's why I can only walk in a straight line and I would like to report a kidnapper. Hello?«

»Young man, listen to me –«

»Mr 2000!« I shouted. »The ALDI kidnapper who abducted Oskar, the one without the helmet! I know where he lives! Please, you have to believe me!«

There was a quiet whistle from the telephone as though somebody was breathing out very slowly in an effort not to lose patience. Who knows how many people called him

---

to dial – Telefonnummer wählen

every day, I thought, to report Mr 2000, when they were really just playing a trick on the police? I might die because of them!

»Really?« said the man finally. »Where are you, lad?«

»Mr 2000 lives at Dieffenbachstrasse 93 in Kreuzberg,« I said very slowly and very clearly and very **proudly**. »On the fourth floor, in the front building on the left or the right. Mr Lake. I mean, he's really called East … No, Westlake. Simon Westlake!«

I took a deep breath. For a while I didn't hear anything, perhaps the compass points had confused the emergency man, too. Then an angry voice said: »Listen, young man. I can see your number on my display! If you call here again wasting our time –«

DISPLAY: A lighty-up thing that shows all kinds of stuff, like phone numbers for example or the price at the cash desk in the supermarket or the title of the film in the DVD player. It's a funny word and I don't really know why every-body uses it. You could just as well say lighty-up thing.

proudly – stolz

I couldn't believe it. I put the phone down quickly without letting the man finish. I should have known from the start no one would believe me. At least nobody could complain that I hadn't tried. But it didn't really get me any further either.

Keep calm, Rico!

It couldn't be all that difficult to concentrate a bit and think properly. Seeing as how I was trapped at the RBs, I might as well think about what might happen next with Oskar and Mr Lake. Oskar was, after all, in much bigger danger than before. Mr Lake didn't give a bean for his life. Beans come in **tins**, so maybe he was keeping Oskar in a tin factory.

Rubbish.

Where do you hide somebody that you've kidnapped? It depends on how you treat them. If you make sure they have enough to eat and drink and that there's a toilet nearby, you can keep them quite far away from you because the victims can take care of themselves. But Mr Lake's victims were small children. They could stand in front of a packed fridge and still go thirsty and hungry and **wet themselves** with fear. Then he'd really be in trouble. No, the longer I thought about it, the more convinced I was that Mr Lake was keeping the kidnapped children somewhere nearby, and …

Near him was near me!

---

tin – Dose

to wet themselves – sich einnässen

Good thinking, Rico!

At this point I have to admit that it took me about two hours to work out that last bit. Well, almost three actually. In the meantime I had moved to the RBs' kitchen. Outside it was already **pitch black**. The only light coming through the windows was from the moon. There were no curtains and I didn't dare put the light on. Once he realised that I hadn't been to the police, Mr Lake would certainly be looking out for me.

I drank some water from the tap and searched the kitchen for something to eat. I knew that the fridge was empty, but I looked inside again all the same. Nothing. In a cupboard I found a packet of pasta, but the RBs' gas cooker has so many knobs and buttons it scares me. You could set out to boil an egg and suddenly the whole flat might blow up around your ears. So I opened the packet of pasta and sucked one piece after another, looking out at the building behind and waiting for the ghost of Miss Bonhöfer to appear, looking for her ashtray.

The pasta felt crinkly in my mouth. Rigatoni, I concluded, without any excitement. With a sad feeling in my stomach I thought about how chubby Thorben had probably thrown the piece of pasta out of the window of his room or over the roof terrace railing before the RBs had gone away. It was just the kind of thing he'd do. Everything had begun with that piece of pasta and now everything would

---

pitch black – tiefschwarz

end with a final piece of pasta which Mr Lake would shove into my cut-off ear.

On the third floor of the rear building, Miss Bonhöfer's shadowier shadow marched past one of the windows in her old flat. I spat out the piece of rigatoni and stared over, too shocked to really be afraid. I had never seen a shadowier shadow so clearly. It came from one side, let's say from the right, moved to the other side, that must be the left, vanished for a while, came back and disappeared in the same direction it had come from in the first place, which must be … left?

It doesn't matter. The shadowier shadow disappeared. And something clicked inside me. At first I thought it was the lottery balls, which up until then had been strangely quiet. But this felt and sounded different. It felt and sounded as though a few **pieces of a jigsaw puzzle** that up until now had been waiting patiently had just fallen into place.

Now I knew everything.

Well, almost everything.

In any case, I knew what I had to do next.

---

piece of a jigsaw puzzle – Puzzelstück

ALMOST THURSDAY

IN THE BUILDING BEHIND OURS

Once I'd got through the partition, I found Mr Marrak's roof-terrace door wide open. Even so, Mr Marrak's flat smelt stale and of old socks. His girlfriend must have used a really awful washing powder. From the hall, I peeped through the slightly open bedroom door. Mr Marrak was alone in bed. His silhouette was moving steadily up and down. He was **snoring**.

SILHOUETTE: Outline or shape. Whoever thought up such a mish-mash of letters? Precisely! The French! I've held a grudge against the French ever since Jule said they were good kissers. They also eat frogs, snails and things, and probably right before kissing too. Yuk!

My heart was in my mouth. It had been almost impossible to squeeze myself through the rustling bamboo canes of the partition on the roof terrace. Then I had almost broken my neck when I slid on the slippery **spiral staircase** down to Mr Marrak's flat and only just managed to hang on to the **handrail**. The moon was high in the sky, but as it was shin-

to snore – schnarchen

spiral staircase – Wendeltreppe

handrail – Geländer

ing almost four hundred thousand kilometres away, it was nearly as dark in here as it was in the cellar of Dieffe 93.

The cellar …

That was the way – and I was almost certain of it now – that Mr Lake moved his victims into the locked building behind ours without being noticed. The basements of the two buildings were connected. Residents aren't actually allowed to go down there – there's water everywhere. Nothing makes me as frightened as water. That's why I only peeked into the cellar once, with Mum, right after we had moved into Dieffe. Dim light from a single, bare bulb. Damp air. A disgusting smell and dripping noises that sounded as though they came from bottomless pits. No thank you!

Mr Lake must have unloaded the children from the boot of his car and dragged them into the building after they had been knocked **unconscious** and all **trussed up** so that nobody noticed them, maybe in a large suitcase or a big laundry bag like Mr Marrak's. Then past Mommsen's ground-floor flat into the cellar, through the pitch-black splish-splash and everything else, and finally up into the building behind ours where he kept the children prisoner on the third floor until their ransom money had been paid. Mr Lake stuck sticky tape over their mouths or gagged them with stinky old hankies so that they couldn't scream. And whenever he went to see them to take them something to

---

unconscious – ohnmächtig

to truss up sb. – jmd. fesseln

eat or to let them go to the toilet and things, the shadowier shadows crept past the windows in Miss Bonhöfer's flat.

That's how far I'd got with my thinking while sucking on pieces of pasta. But then there was a **gap** – something was missing, and this something wouldn't give me any peace. It was to do with forwards or backwards, with right or left, with before or after, but I simply couldn't work it out. At one point the lottery machine in my head had been drumming so hard that I feared the RBs would return from their holiday to find me on their kitchen table with an overcooked brain. A fine mess. So I'd given up.

My eyes got used to the darkness in Mr Marrak's flat faster than I expected. I left my search of the bedroom for last – that was the most dangerous place with Mr Marrak in there snoring. Hopefully I would find what I was looking for in one of the other rooms. I felt my way all over the place at a snail's pace. Nothing – but then …

I hadn't thought there'd be anything of interest in the bathroom, but when there were no other rooms left, I thought I might as well take a look. It was a kind of excuse not to go into the bedroom yet. The tiled floor was covered in splashes of water. Mr Marrak had had a shower before going to bed. At least that was something, I thought, even if he's still a pig because he doesn't air his pongy flat properly. His work clothes were scattered all over the floor in messy piles. I almost cried out for joy: his large bunch of safety

---

gap – Lücke

keys was hanging from the trouser belt! I unclipped it as carefully as possible so that none of the hundred keys began to clink. A few of them didn't feel like keys at all. More like pieces of metal with all sorts of bits and pieces sticking out of them. Probably for opening safes and things like that. But it was the normal keys I needed.

Outside, in front of the low door to the white-covered stairway on Mr Marrak's roof terrace, I held my breath, trying out key after key. After about twenty of them, I found the right one and finally the door swung open. I was standing at the top of the stairs that led down into the building behind ours.

I was already **drenched** in sweat.

A nasty cold filled the stairway. I shivered. It was as though somebody had opened a tomb. The further down the worn-out stairs I went, the more creepy it felt. The stairs, covered in white **mould**, creaked and groaned under my unsteady feet. Slime-oozing worms wriggled their way out of the dirty, damp walls and the groaning of long-lost souls clawed

---

to drench – durchnässen

mould – Schimmel

its way into my eardrums from the **torture chambers** under the deep cellar.

Well maybe not: that's what it was like in a horror film that Mrs Dahling brought home once by mistake. I thought it was great and really wanted to watch to the end, unlike Mrs Dahling who kept her face hidden behind one of her soft cushions the whole time and only came out occasionally to grab another canapés. I didn't know why she made such a fuss. When *Musikantenstadl* was on, she watched all of it.

It really was very cold and dark in the stairway because of the boarded-up windows. It was as though somebody had tied a scarf around my eyes, but I wasn't afraid. Well, all right, I was a bit. The important thing was to be careful not to think about anything creepy. That was easy. In the last few hours I'd done so much thinking that my head felt like a washing machine on the spin cycle and there was no way I could do any more. What I really had to make sure of was that I didn't take a wrong step in the dark. There was a reason why this building had been locked up after the gas explosion. Oskar had said that »in danger of collapse« meant that every stair under my feet and every bit of wall I leaned against could break as soon as I touched it.

On the other hand, Mr Lake couldn't have had any problems. And he'd had to come up from the cellar every time;

---

torture chamber – Folterkammer

it wasn't as far for me. I reached the fifth floor quite quickly, and it was only a couple of floors down to the third.

More fiddling with the keys. I knew that would happen. That was the most difficult part, without a torch or any other light, but this time it was even quicker than up on the roof. Just a few tries, and suddenly I was in dead Miss Bonhöfer's flat. The bunch of keys from Mr Marrak's **security business** was brilliant!

I pressed the door shut behind me and called out Oskar's name quietly and nervously. No reply. He had to be hidden in one of the back rooms. He was probably lying in a corner full of straw, gagged and out cold.

The flat was totally empty. No furniture, no ghosts, nothing. It smelled of dust and **soot**, and the slight scent of those pretty, small lilac flowers floated in the air. Violets. That had to be Miss Bonhöfer's perfume. It had not only survived the gas explosion and the fire in the flat, but all the years that had gone by since then, too. The thought made me really sad for some reason.

I crept through the hall, past a toilet, the kitchen and the first room. Nothing and nobody inside. From the outside, a pale light fell through the dirty window panes. I nearly had a heart attack when I thought I saw Mr Lake in his brightly lit kitchen in the front building across the yard. But there was no sign of the monster himself, just steam rising from a

---

security business – Sicherheitsfirma

soot – Ruß

small pan on the cooker. Mr Lake surely wouldn't have left that alone if he intended to check up on Oskar. But maybe he was cooking him something to eat.

I had to get a move on.

In Mr Fitzke's flat, the flat opposite Mr Lake's, the curtains were drawn. A light was shining behind them. I wondered what the old stinker was doing. Probably counting his collection of kids' heads.

I walked along to the end of the hall to where a door led to the two rooms at the back of the flat.

Locked.

Try the keys.

Success after lots of – well about nine – tries.

Door open and in we go.

Now I could see my own room through the window. It was below me and a little bit to one side. It was dark of course, but the creepy thought occurred to me that the light might suddenly go on down there and I would see Rico looking over at me, scared, from his window, because at that moment he could see my shadowier shadow.

Oh God, oh God!

If I were Mr Lake, I would have taken the window out or boarded it up, I thought. Then I realised that everybody in the front building would have noticed. So it was better to wait for **the cover of the night** and to play shadowier

---

the cover of the night – der Schutz der Nacht

shadows. And up until now it had worked perfectly. What a sneaky man!

»Oskar?«

Still no answer.

I was getting more and more nervous. I was slowly running out of rooms. But not out of keys. I figured out the next door in a flash. The fact that it was locked made me hopeful. I pushed it open carefully. Pitch-black blackity blackness. The little moonlight that came from the connecting room wasn't enough to light the furthest corners of the space.

»Oskar?«

I stepped in blindly, five, six steps. Then two things happened at once: Miss Bonhöfer's violet scent turned into the smell of a **quarter pounder** with cheese. And I banged my knee and my forehead so hard against a wall that I gave a muffled shout and swore.

»You found my aeroplane, didn't you?« said a quiet voice.

My knee and forehead were forgotten straight away. I grinned so widely with relief that I thought the corners of my mouth would meet over my head.

»But only by chance,« I answered. »It was in the rubbish bin.«

»And after that you went to see Sophia.«

»Yes, but she didn't tell me anything. She was afraid for you. I worked out everything myself, by thinking.«

---

quarter pounder – Burger mit extra viel Fleisch

Well, almost everything. Later I could tell him about the clue Sophia didn't realise she'd given me, the one about the jingle-jangle man. For now it was enough being able to really impress Oskar.

»I'm glad you're here,« said his voice. »Where did you get the key from?«

»Stole it from Mr Marrak.«

»Very clever. OK, now lock the door again.«

»Why?«

»Because there's a contact switch built into it. The light only goes on when the door is closed and locked, so no one outside can see it.«

»I didn't know there were things like that.«

»It's similar to a fridge, just the other way round.«

Imagining something the other way round is always very difficult, especially when you have difficulties imagining it the right away round. »Are you trying to say,« I thought out loud, »that there's no light on in a fridge when it's closed?«

Oskar gave a quiet groan.

»Are you hurt?« I asked.

»Just lock the door,« came the reply.

It took a while, and a dangerous amount of jangling, until I found the key I had come in with. Oskar waited without saying another word.

When the light finally went on I saw through scrunched-up eyes that he was crouching on an old, worn-out mattress, surrounded by a load of plastic bags and McDonald's wrappers and **dozens** of empty Coke bottles. What a **pigsty**! Mr Lake had put large cushions against the wall. They looked as though they were filled with cotton wool. The ceiling was covered in them, too, and a lonely energy-saving light bulb was dangling down from the middle. I'd seen things like this in thrillers. **Padded** cells to stop the noise – if you shouted in here, nobody outside could hear you.

The cushions were light green. *The green room*, I thought, and for the first time since I'd set off, an ice-cold shiver ran down my spine.

Oskar himself looked **spotless**. Well, he'd only been locked in here since yesterday. But somehow I had pictured him in torn clothes, with a dirty face and things. Without his blue helmet he looked strangely a bit helpless, and his sticky-out ears were really unbelievably big, but that was it. The only unusual thing was that he was fastened to the wall above him by a short chain and a cuff around one of his wrists. The chain was so short he couldn't lie down. He would even have to sleep sitting up.

That was the second cold shiver.

I looked around for a toilet. There had to be one somewhere, otherwise the room wouldn't have smelled of cheeseburgers, but of **wee**.

---

dozen – Dutzend

pigsty – Schweinestall

to pad – auspolstern

spotless – makellos

wee – Pipi

»It's out there in the hall, behind the front door,« Oskar said as though he had read my thoughts. »It's just as sound-proof as this room.«

So it was just as I had thought. Whenever Mr Lake had taken a child to the toilet, the shadowier shadows had crept through Miss Bonhöfer's flat!

Oskar beamed at me with his green eyes and his large, unbrushed teeth – another thing Mr Lake should have on his **conscience** – and all at once I felt the way an older brother must feel. My face went bright red with pride. I had saved Oskar! Or nearly, at least.

»What kind of chain is that?«

»Quality steel, I would say,« said Oskar. »Probably **unalloyed**, which means it has less than 0.8 per cent **manganese** and 0.5 per cent silicon. If the **percentage** of either was higher, the –«

»Stop! How do I get it off you?«

He raised his right arm. »The key is with the rest.«

»With the rest of what?«

»The rest of the keys. The ones in your hand.«

»Why didn't you say so?«

Normally I would have been angry, but I swallowed it. You probably get a little crabby if you're forced to eat doz-

---

conscience – Gewissen

to alloy – legieren

manganese – Managan

percentage – Prozentsatz

ens of hamburgers and cheeseburgers and that sort of stuff. Before I could embarrass myself by stupidly asking how on earth Oskar could have put away so much food and above all so much Coke in such a short space of time without brown stuff running out of his nose, I realised that the rubbish must have come from all six victims.

This thought bothered me somehow – I suddenly had that same **nagging feeling** the lottery balls in my head had rolled around in the wrong direction between the front and the back, the right and the left, the before and the after. But it was just as hard to figure it out as it had been the last time, even harder in fact, because this time I had to concentrate on setting Oskar free.

I quickly found the key – it was the smallest of them all – and unlocked the handcuff. Oskar slipped it off and rubbed his wrist. When he got up from the mattress, his knees cracked and a tiny groan of pain slipped out of his mouth.

»Did you just sit around the whole time?« I asked.

»What do you mean just?« He looked at his sore wrist and an angry, horizontal line appeared on his forehead.

»Sitting is a very complicated matter.«

---

nagging feeling – nagendes Gefühl

ALMOST THURSDAY AGAIN

THE ESCAPE

Dear Mr Wehmeyer,

I don't want to hear any complaints about the diary getting serious at this point! The following events were dramatic, and you should be happy that they even let me write my diary in the hospital.

It's time for you to start thinking about my bonus.

Yours sincerelier,

Frederico Doretti

Walking seemed to be less complicated than sitting, or at least Oskar didn't complain. Through the window in one of the front rooms I checked that there was still a light on in Mr Lake's flat. There was. You could even see the **child-chopper-upper**. He was getting himself something to drink from the fridge and talking on his mobile phone. He was probably being rude to Oskar's dad again. All the better. If Oskar and I didn't make the building collapse, we could clear off unnoticed and tell the police. They would probably believe Oskar if he stood in front of them as large as life, unlike me. We just had to get a move on before Mr Lake remembered his beans.

---

child-chopper-upper – Kinderzerschnibbler

Once we were in the boarded-up stairway, we held on to each other's hands. It was as black as coal again. As I took the first step up to the little white house on the roof, Oskar pulled me back with a start. It was strange to hear his voice without seeing him.

»Have you gone mad?« he hissed. »We'll run right into him if we go that way!«

»We'll run right into him if we go down there,« I answered. »He comes up through the cellar after all.«

»Which cellar?«

»The one he brought you up through.«

Maybe it was the darkness that was making Oskar so slow to understand. Maybe, I thought, child prodigies are only really clever when it's light.

»Why should he bring me through the cellar?« Oskar said.

»Because he's got no other way of getting into the rear building.«

»You got here!«

Slowly this was getting on my nerves. While we were **babbling** on here, Mr Lake might be drawing closer.

»I came through Mr Marrak's roof terrace,« I explained, forcing myself to be patient. »Through the little white stairway house, don't you remember? With Mr Marrak's keys. How is Mr Lake supposed to get hold of those?«

»Mr Lake?« Oskar's voice sounded clueless. »What's this got to do with Mr Lake?«

---

to babble – schwatzen

And that was the third shiver down my back. It was also the third time I got the feeling that I had gone in the wrong direction with my thoughts somewhere – but now it was no longer a nagging feeling but a feeling that sank its teeth into me and wouldn't let go. I was a complete idiot! I was the biggest child proddity of all the child proddities in the world! My mistake had nothing to do with right or left, forward and back. It was a mistake with before and after: Mr Lake had only been living at Dieffe 93 for a week! But I had seen the shadowier shadows much, much earlier – the first time had been a few months ago when the kidnappings had begun. Why and how would Mr Lake have brought his victims here?

Suddenly a light went on in my head.

»It's not Mr Lake – it's Mr Marrak!« I whispered in horror. »Alarms, Safes and Locks … Sales, Service and something or other!«

»That's how I tracked him down,« said Oskar. »Sophia remembered his jangling bunch of keys. And his red work uniform with the golden safe on it.«

»And Sophia,« I said. »How did you find her?«

»I asked around for her at all the primary schools in Tempelhof.«

»Why her? Why not one of the other children?«

»She was the second victim. And there were photos in the newspapers. Sophia looked like she would talk if she knew anything.«

»The bunch of keys and the red uniform,« I repeated quietly. »Mr Marrak. Oh God, oh God! Sophia should have told the police!«

»She was afraid!«

»She's still afraid. But then you should have told the police.«

Oskar was quiet. I could picture him talking to Sophia. How Sophia told him things you would only tell another child. How she gave Oskar her little red aeroplane, happy that she finally had somebody to talk to. How Oskar, just as happy, pinned on the aeroplane, a little boy with a blue helmet on his head who normally didn't have any friends because he was too clever.

»I promised her I wouldn't tell,« Oskar murmured. »My mum always said you shouldn't break promises.«

I swallowed. Something was pressing against my shoulders and my heart as though the darkness was **crushing** us. »And then?« I whispered.

»Then I copied out contact details for all the **locksmiths** in Berlin from the phone book,« Oskar continued. »Every afternoon after school I went to look for them, one by one. It took weeks. I eventually found Mr Marrak by chance. The phone book only has his mobile number, not his address. He dropped in at another locksmith that I happened to be watching. Maybe he was visiting a friend. I was standing on the other side of the street and saw him getting out

---

to crush – zerdrücken

locksmith – Schlosser

and knew I had him. At least almost. He didn't stay long. But long enough for me **to hail a taxi** and follow him.«

»Hey, I took a taxi too!«

»But you didn't get thrown out halfway, did you? The stupid driver turned to me at a red light and wanted to know if I could pay. I didn't have enough money with me and he refused to go any further. That was in Urbanstrasse. I could see Mr Marrak **indicating** ahead and turning off into Grimmstrasse, so I followed him on foot. His car was parked in Dieffenbachstrasse, but I didn't know which apartment block he'd disappeared into. I waited. About two hours later he left number 93. There were two possibilities. Either he has just visited a customer …«

»… or he lived there,« I said. »That's right, isn't it? And you crept around Dieffenbachstrasse to find out. And that's when you met me.«

I couldn't see Oskar but I could tell that he was nodding. I also had a bitter taste in my mouth.

»You used me to get into the building! To look for Mr Marrak! To find out if he lived here!«

No answer again. I didn't say anything else either. Silence spread like a jet-black puddle. We should have been getting out of there. Instead we were standing in a stairway that was in danger of collapse, unable to see our own hands in front of our faces and not knowing what to say – me because of

---

to hail a taxi – ein Taxi anhalten

to indicate – hier: den Blinker anmachen

disappointment and Oskar because he didn't know how to say sorry.

»In the beginning,« he said finally and was quiet again for a second. »In the beginning I didn't care about you. I really just wanted to get into the building. But up on the roof terrace –«

»– where you finally found what you wanted –«

»– I was sorry that I'd used you. I like you, Rico! You were never mean to me, and you risked your life to find me. You're my only friend.« His last words were a whisper: »You're risking your life right now.«

I grumbled a little bit. I didn't have another friend apart from Oskar. It's strange how people have just as little an idea of what to do with somebody who's not that bright as they do with somebody who's really intelligent. I thought of the afternoon on the roof terrace and how Oskar had held my hand. That had been lovely, and not a lie at all. I had felt it.

»How did you get yourself kidnapped?« I said, finally.

I heard him breathe out with relief. »That was simple. I had planned it for Tuesday morning, but then I changed my mind because I'd promised to visit you.«

»Without your helmet?« I said, hardly able to believe it.

»I'm not as afraid when you're with me,« Oskar murmured quietly and carried on speaking quickly as though it was embarrassing. »I took the underground to Kottbusser Tor and went towards Dieffenbachstrasse. But in Grimmstrasse Mr Marrak was coming in my direction and got into his car.«

I felt all dizzy. I had seen Mr Marrak going out of the building from the living-room window! He must have **bumped into** Oskar, or Oskar into him, not a minute later.

»I couldn't miss the opportunity!« Oskar said. »So I asked him if he could take me with him – told him that my dad hadn't come home from the pub last night and I wanted to go and look for him and um, you know ... The kind of things you dream up on the spot.«

Or if it's really happened to you, I thought.

»He took me with him in any case. We only went past three traffic lights. By then I had made sure to give him Dad's phone number and Mr Marrak sprayed something into my face. I didn't wake up until the afternoon when he pulled me out of the laundry bag in his flat. I was handcuffed and tied up and a bit fuzzy in the head, but I had –«

»You were in his laundry bag?«

»I think so. That's what it looked like.«

I didn't know what upset me more: that Mr Marrak, after **drugging** Oskar in the morning and somehow tying him up without being noticed, had gone about his work perfectly calmly until the afternoon. Or that I had met him on the stairs and talked to him while Oskar had been **bundled up** in a bag at our feet. That part, I decided, I would only

---

to bump into – hier: jmd. zufällig treffen

to drug – betäuben

to bundle up – zusammenbündeln

tell Oskar much later. I was really shocked by that – not to mention the fact that Mr Marrak probably didn't have a girlfriend who did his washing or anything like that.

»But in the meantime I had almost managed to somehow get one arm free,« Oskar carried on. »And when Mr Marrak dragged me over to the little white house on his roof terrace, I recognised it, tore the red aeroplane off my shirt without him noticing and threw it over the railing.«

»But why? Mr Marrak would have freed you once your dad had paid the ransom, if not before. Then you could have been a **witness** against him and everybody would have had to believe you.«

For a while, all I could hear was Oskar breathing. »I wasn't sure,« he finally said quietly, »whether my dad would … whether he would get the money together quickly enough. Stuff like that.«

The last sentence sounded **desperately sad** as though Oskar wasn't sure if his dad would have paid the ransom money for him at all.

»And if that was the case,« he said, still quietly, »you were my only hope. There was only a tiny, little chance but it was obviously big enough.«

There was another silence.

»A long story,« a voice rang out above us. »But thank you for the revealing explanation!«

---

to witness – bezeugen

desperately sad – extrem traurig

A torch flashed on and dazzled us.

Oskar and I screamed at the same time. We ran at the same time too – down the stairs. Mr Marrak, who had been listening to us from a few steps further up, **thundered** after us, which was lucky in a funny way, because his torch lit up the way not only for him but for us too. We jumped and crashed our way through the building and I decided whoever had said it was in danger of collapse was completely stupid – it was clearly bombproof.

At the bottom of the stairs, we stood in front of the door that led out to the backyard. I pressed the bunch of keys into Oskar's hand. He was cleverer than I was.

»You do it!« I hissed. »I'll talk to him!«

Mr Marrak crashed down behind us like somebody who'd taken a running jump into a swimming pool and found it was empty. His torch fell to the ground with a bang and rolled away. Dust flew up into the air. In the beam of light from the floor I could see Oskar standing next to me without moving as though now was the moment he had chosen to try out how it felt to be a tree or a traffic light or something. I think it's called being frozen with fear. Behind him, three shadows were stuck to the wall, two small ones and one giant one.

»End of the line!« said Mr Marrak.

If you could weigh anger, then his weighed at least a ton or even more. A lot, in any case. I had no idea how I was

---

to thunder – donnern

going to stop him to give us some time and to unfreeze Oskar. But I would have to think of something. I could feel the lottery machine slowly starting up. If I waited five more seconds, it would be too late. So I threw him the first best question I could think of, like throwing a bone at a **guard dog**, though I would rather have asked it really casually, over a cup of hot chocolate or something. Preferably while there were bars between us, with him in a **maximum-security prison**.

»Why did you phone Oskar's dad after the kidnapping instead of writing him a letter like you usually do?«

Mr Marrak glared at me nastily, but his answer shot out as though from a gun. »To hurry things up,« he growled. »So that I could get rid of this irritating **super-smarty-pants** as fast as possible!«

Oskar didn't even bat an eyelid in his deep freeze as the **brawny** face of his kidnapper pushed right in front of his.

»You are the weirdest and most irritating child I have ever come across!« Mr Marrak snorted at him. »Do you know how they would have treated you in the Middle Ages? Like a freak! Like a punishment from God! Brats like you would have been burned at the stake four hundred years ago!«

---

guard dog – Wachhund

maximum-security prison – Hochsicherheitsgefängnis

super-smarty-pants – Super-Klugscheißer

brawny – bullig

»The Middle Ages,« Oskar said scornfully, »ended more than five hundred years ago. The Renaissance began after that, you **ignoramus**!«

I hadn't heard of the Renaissance, but it must have been terrible because Mr Marrak winced. For a moment, I was afraid he would hit Oskar. Instead he put on the sweetest face of all time. In crime thrillers that's always a sign that the criminal's **gone loopy** and **has bats in the belfry**. Mr Marrak, and I was one hundred per cent certain of this, didn't even have a belfry.

»I actually like children!« he said in a sugary-sweet voice. »I really like them, in fact. But their parents should keep a closer eye on them, that's all I ever wanted. It's a bad world out there. I didn't care about the money. Yes, yes, it's true, I like children. Even educationally challenged ones!«

Now he spun around with a jerk and turned to me. Over his shoulder I was relieved to see that Oskar had finally started to move as though he had only been waiting to show off a bit with the Renaissance before he got going. He began to fiddle with the lock carefully and without making a sound.

»But I like my freedom too!« Mr Marrak breathed right into my face. His grin was as **lopsided** as though somebody

---

ignoramus – Dummkopf

to go loopy – (ugs.) durchdrehen

to have bats in the belfry – einen Vogel/Dachschaden haben

lopsided – schief

had sliced a clown's mask in two, right down the middle. »You shouldn't have stuck your nosy nose into my business, Rico Doretti! Now I'm afraid I'll have to cut it off.«

He took a step towards me.

I wrinkled my brow.

That wasn't right.

»You're doing it in the wrong **order**,« I said.

Mr Marrak paused, puzzled. »Which order?«

»The cutting-off bit. The ears come first.« I began to list everything, mightily proud that I'd remembered everything Felix had told me.

»Kidnappers always cut the ears off first. Both of them. Then one hand, and then –«

»You stupid little –«

»Please don't interrupt me!«

Honestly, when you finally remember something, someone like that comes along! I was so angry that I carried on shouting.

»And then the arm that belongs to it! The other one has to stay on so that you can still write begging letters! But I'll tell you right away, the most my mum can do is crack open the piggy bank for you! And, well … that's it!«

It felt really good to shout at Mr Marrak even though I must admit that what I had to say wasn't particularly sensible. If he wasn't going to get anything out of Mum, he could saw off both my arms before moving on to the legs.

---

order – Reihenfolge

Luckily for me, however, he had no time to think of that himself.

Behind me, there was a click.

The door flew open. Pale, milky moonlight poured into the stairway. I shot past Mr Marrak like a **bolt of lightning**.

If Oskar hadn't been so small, I might not have tripped over him. I have no idea why he didn't sprint off at the same time. He could even have had a head start, but he seemed to be waiting for me. I bowled right into him in the middle of the doorway.

Both of us fell. I crashed into the backyard next to Oskar and slid over the rough, hard ground on one forearm. I could feel it starting to bleed. Then something heavy hit me in the stomach and there was a shout as Mr Marrak tripped over me and fell to the ground like a tree that had been **chopped down**. Next to me Oskar got to his feet and stretched out a hand towards me. I grabbed it and got up with a groan.

»Quick, let's go!« I coughed.

We took off again, Oskar in front of me, with screams that would have torn the Greek hero O – that's the one with the wooden horse and the besieged wife – from his ship's mast. I was quicker than Oskar and overtook him to reach the large door to our building first.

The large sticking door!

---

bolt of lightning – Blitzschlag

to chop down – fällen

I pressed both hands down on the handle and pulled with all my strength on the bit that was supposed to open, but it barely moved, three or four centimetres at most! The crack that opened up was too small even for Oskar to slip through.

I spun round, the hard door at my back. Oskar pressed himself against me, his arms around my waist. In the moonlight I could see that Mr Marrak had got back on his feet. He stared at us with wild eyes then charged like a **raving mad** bull.

»Police!« cried a voice above us. My head shot up. Up above, on the fourth floor, Mr Lake was standing in the window, a pistol in his outstretched right hand. »Don't move or I'll have to shoot!«

But Mr Marrak had already caught up with us. He **reared up** above Oskar and me like a mountain. I covered Oskar's head with my arms to protect him, then stared right into Mr Marrak's eyes. Unfortunately, Mum and Oskar are a lot better at the staring trick than I am. It didn't work one bit.

The last thing I heard was a loud roar. The last thing I saw were two things coming down from the sky, one above me and one above Mr Marrak. What came down on me was Mr Marrak's fist. It hit me right on the forehead and, as I slowly fell over and everything went black, Mr Marrak made a strange face, grabbed his bleeding forehead and fell over too.

---

raving mad – tobsüchtig

to rear up – sich aufbäumen

Millions of years later I woke up. I was being carried through the hallway in our block of flats. I looked up and saw Mr Lake's face. I was in his arms. Somebody was holding the front door open, probably the caretaker, Mr Mommsen. Somebody was sobbing, probably Mrs Dahling. Somebody was babbling on in excitement about something, probably Oskar. Flashing red and blue lights lit up the street in front of Dieffenbachstrasse 93, but I was still looking up at Mr Lake. It was like in a dream. I could hear my own voice murmuring, and Mr Lake held me close to his chest and listened to every word.

»One day my dad went out in a boat with friends, off the coast of Naples. It was a stormy autumn day. The waves were high and black and **foamy**. My dad threw out a **fishing line**. A very large fish took a bite; a huge struggle broke out. The fish won. It pulled Dad overboard. My dad drowned in the deep blue sea.«

---

foamy – schäumend

fishing line – Angelleine

THURSDAY

BRIGHT AND SUNNY

Mum has just visited me in the hospital. Nobody else has been allowed in yet: not Mr Lake, not Mrs Dahling, not Berts. Not Mr Kiesling or Mommsen either, even though it's nice that both of them have asked about me. They won't even let Oskar in; I won't see him until tomorrow. And all because of a little bump on the head!

»The press is waiting down there.« Mum was standing at the window of my single room looking out. »They're **queuing** up as far back as the canal.«

»Will I be famous now?«

She sighed. »There's no way around it. You and Oskar. But only for a few days. We live in a fast world that forgets fast.«

When she first came in and took me carefully in her arms without saying a word, I had started to cry right away. She was wearing black clothes which made her look as dark midnight, and her face looked very worried. I thought it was all my fault. But that wasn't true. Uncle Christian had died the day before. I knew that Mum hadn't got on well with him, but he was her brother all the same.

Mum had come to Berlin because of me, though she would have to go back down to the bottom and left again, because of the funeral and everything. I felt really sorry for her, but I was happy that Uncle Christian would lie in his coffin without me after all. I was sure it would be more comfortable for him that way too.

---

to queue – Schlange stehen

»Do you know what the crazy thing is?« Mum said and came over from the window to sit on the edge of my bed. »The crazy thing is that Christian **bequeathed** everything to me. He didn't have anybody else. It's sad somehow, don't you think?«

»What does bequeath mean?«

»He left everything to us. The money, the car – everything.«

»Are we rich now?«

»Depends on how you look at it. He had a house too ...«

»Do we have to move house now?« I called out in fear.

»We don't have to.« Mum stroked my bandaged arm. She looked deep into my eyes. »But we will.«

That was the last straw! It's difficult to think when you've got **concussion**. But something inside me thought all by itself: If I had to move to the bottom and left on the map, then I would lose Oskar as a friend, and Mrs Dahling and the canapés too. That I would have to go to another school before Mr Wehmeyer had read my holiday diary. That it would never work out with Mr Lake and Mum and that there was definitely no bingo club at the bottom and left. How could Mum have made such a decision without talking to me about it? I looked at her, horrified, and wondered what there was to grin about.

---

to bequeath sth. to sb. – jmd. etw. vermachen, vererben

concussion – Gehirnerschütterung

»You know, I hear,« she said very slowly, »that in a certain building in Dieffenbachstrasse there'll be an empty flat available very soon. Up on the fifth floor. With a roof terrace. The view over Berlin is supposed to be phenomenal.«

It took me a little time, and then I realised what she meant.

»We can live above Mr Lake!« I burst out.

»Yes, Rico. Directly above a policeman.«

It was still terribly embarrassing to me that I had got it so wrong about Mr Lake. But how could I have known that he wasn't only a police inspector, but also in charge of the kidnappings?

That's why he'd been able to put six red dots on the map before the public was told about Oskar's kidnapping. That's why he'd been talking to Oskar's stupid dad and had told him off on the mobile. And that's why the man on the emergency number had thought I was having him on – I had tried to tell him that the kidnapper was the police inspector in charge of the investigation. Really, you wouldn't even be able to think that up with a normal brain! Well, maybe Miss Marple would have figured it out; she's a lot cleverer than I am. But my bottom is nowhere near as big as hers, and from now on I can ask Mr Lake for help if anybody else gets kidnapped.

»Do you still think he's the hottest thing you've ever met in your entire life?« I asked Mum carefully.

Maybe I should have left it, because suddenly there it was again, the mixture of tiredness and sadness on her face that had been there in the thinking chair after Mr Lake's visit on Monday. Only this time there was a very small smile too. And even though Mum did not reply and only kissed the bandage on my forehead when she said goodbye, I felt a little bit of hope come back.

Well, that's it. Holiday time for my holiday diary. I have to take a break so that the lottery machine can sort itself out. I wrote all of the last bit by hand, in the notebook I asked Mum to bring.

Next week, when I'm let out of hospital, Mr Wehmeyer says I have to copy it all over to the computer, because of my **orthography**.

> ORTHOGRAPHY: Means spelling in complicated speak. It's no wonder I find it difficult, because it's got the word GRAPH in it, so it's like maths, which I've already told you isn't my strong point.

---

orthography – Rechtschreibung

I have to get a move on, because it's nearly dinner time and if Sister Leonie finds out that I've spent the whole afternoon writing away secretly, there'll be trouble. She's great and very pretty too, like a mixture of Jule and Cindy the nail technician, even though I haven't seen her boobs yet. So I'll put the notebook away. I've actually told everything there is to tell.

Apart from one thing.

Apparently Mr Fitzke kept a boulder in his stinky flat, which is what hit Mr Marrak right on the forehead the night he was chasing us, but the biggest question is why were there *hundreds of other stones* lying in it, large and small? That's what the police found when they questioned him.

But Mr Fitzke didn't want to tell anybody why, not even Mr Lake, even though he's a neighbour, and not the people from the newspapers and the television, even though Mr Fitzke is a hero now, like Oskar and me. Mr Fitzke of all people! He grumbled that it wasn't against the law to keep stones in your flat, and he's probably right. I'm just pleased it wasn't a kid's head he chucked down into the yard that night. All the same I think Mr Fitzke has a secret. No normal person collects stones and throws the biggest one out of the window in the middle of the night, and Mr Fitzke said it wasn't to hit Mr Marrak or us two boys screaming our heads off and **disturbing** his peace and quiet, but *for other reasons*!

---

to disturb – stören

Oh God!
Maybe I should tell Oskar about it tomorrow.
Yes, I'll definitely tell Oskar about it tomorrow.

THE END

FREUNDSCHAFT GEGEN VORURTEILE

Andreas Steinhöfel
HONIGKUCKUCKSKINDER
Taschenbuch
208 Seiten
ISBN 978-3-551-31780-3
Auch als E-Book erhältlich

DIE ZWÖLFJÄHRIGE LENA und ihre Mutter verlieren ihre Wohnung und müssen ins heruntergekommene »Hotel Paradies« am Hafen ziehen, wo Asylbewerber und Obdachlose zusammengepfercht werden. Dort freundet sich Lena mit dem Mädchen Ajoke aus Angola an. Gemeinsam mit dem kleinen Efrem versuchen die beiden dahinterzukommen, wer für die Diebstähle verantwortlich ist, die sich in letzter Zeit im Haus ereignen. Doch die Ausmaße des Betrugs sind größer als gedacht und die Spur führt zum Besitzer und Aufseher, Herrn Schmuck …